DREAMING OF HER SECRET SANTA'S KISS

Cowboy Mountain Christmas
Book 3

JESSIE GUSSMAN

Contents

Acknowledgments

Cover art by Lara Wynter
Editing by Heather Hayden
Narration by Jay Dyess
Author Services by CE Author Assistant

Listen to the unabridged audio for FREE performed by Jay Dyess on the Say with Jay channel on YouTube. Get early access to all of Jay's recordings and listen to Jessie's books before they're available to the general public, plus get daily Bible readings by Jay and bonus scenes by becoming a Say with Jay channel member.

Chapter One

Note from Jessie:

Sorry, I know it says "Chapter 1" here, but I wanted to make sure everyone saw this, and sometimes Amazon opens your kindle directly to Chapter 1, skipping everything before it.

Some of my ARC readers suggested a Trigger Warning for this book.

I thought that was a good idea, but, since I'm a story teller, I thought I'd tell you a story to let you know what might be in this book that could stir up some painful memories and feelings. I don't want you to read this book if it's going to hurt you or make you sad.

Back when I was a young mother I saw an interview on late night TV. I don't usually watch TV, but I'm guessing I was up with one of my babies. Maybe they were sick.

Anyway, some late-night TV host was interviewing a porn star.

I got married young and was a very young mother. That girl on TV was probably exactly my age.

She described some of the things she did, despicable things. Things I had never heard of or imagined. I think she shocked the shock jock as she removed her clothes and offered to do those despicable things to him.

I should have turned the TV off.

But my heart was broken.

Beyond her fake smile and false bravado and her seeming unconcern for any type of decency or modesty lay a soul that my God loved and died for.

To me, her pain was real. I could feel it just as sure as if I were sitting beside her and she were crying on my shoulder. For me, every word that came out of her mouth was a plea for love and acceptance – the kind that only God can give – and she was trying to fill that soul-deep need by any and all depravities known to man.

We were poor. We never had much. But I had been blessed beyond measure.

I knew, as I sat there, my heart hurting, that I could have had a different family, different parents, different school, made different choices, that, but for the grace of God, that girl could have been me.

I don't remember her name, don't know what happened to her. But she made a life-time impression on me, and I wanted to dedicate this book to her. Because she changed my life.

~Jessie Gussman, October 16, 2020

Burgundy Gannon rapped sharply on the dilapidated old farmhouse door, drawing a deep breath and trying to pretend this wasn't her last resort.

She was also trying to pretend her ankle didn't hurt.

She hadn't noticed the weak board on the porch steps a couple seconds ago. When she stepped on it and it gave way, she was unprepared. She didn't think she'd actually sprained her ankle, but it was definitely throbbing.

If she got the job, it would be worth it.

Of course, as run-down as the whole farm looked, maybe she should insist on prepayment.

Was having a job that she ended up not getting paid for better than not having a job at all?

The door opened before she could figure out the answer to that question. She thought it might be a no.

A wizened old lady appeared as the door cracked wider. Wild white hair stuck out in all directions from her head, and she wore bright green pants with an orange flowered shirt and a pink vest.

Black high-top Converse sneakers completed the outfit.

Even in LA, Burgundy's most recent address, this lady would be considered eccentric.

In Mistletoe, Arkansas? She was probably right up there with UFO sightings.

Her eyes looked shrewd, and they were narrowed as they looked Burgundy up and down.

If this lady, Mrs. Scholz, was an inch over four feet, it wasn't by much.

It didn't really matter how tall she was. Her eyes more than made up for any lack in height. It felt like she could see into Burgundy's heart and past and knew exactly what she was trying to hide.

The guilt that never quite completely left her slithered in her stomach, burning.

It always made her want to crumple in on herself.

She straightened her shoulders instead. The sins of her past were covered.

She knew it. Had knowledge. Sometimes, though, it was hard to remember and harder to believe. And even harder to act like it.

"State your business, or get gone."

The words were spit out, and they didn't really have an undertone of kindness in them.

Burgundy blinked, a little taken aback. But she didn't allow her shoulders to drop, nor did she step back.

She'd been in tougher places than this.

Of course, she'd taken worst jobs than this too.

That's why she needed this one so badly. There was always the temptation, no matter how far she was away from her past, to go back to it. If she needed it.

She knew there was something she could do to support herself.

Even if it was reprehensible.

She wanted to think she would die first.

But she knew she wouldn't. She was a survivor, not a martyr.

"Pastor Race sent me. He said you needed a caretaker."

There. Her voice was level, calm. With just the right amount of caring in it. Maybe Hollywood had passed her up, but she was still a good actress.

The woman's eyes narrowed, and her lips pursed, although the wrinkles in her face didn't straighten out. She looked Burgundy up and down, then up and down again.

Once more, Burgundy had that feeling like she'd been found wanting or that she'd been found out.

No one in this town knows what you are. Relax. They won't find out, unless you tell them.

Unless someone watches...

Not in this town. Not in middle America. That's for the big cities.

It wasn't true. She knew it wasn't true. She also knew it was shocking the people who might know her.

But in her movies, she had been a brunette.

For six months, she'd been a redhead.

That's why her hair was now platinum blonde.

She'd also straightened her natural curls out.

The glasses were part of her disguise as well.

"Well? What do you have to say for yourself? Are you just gonna stand there staring at me?"

"Race Steiner sent me. He said you were in need of a caretaker. That's what I am. A caretaker."

She was kind of proud of her acting skills.

She wasn't anything close to a caretaker.

Some of her coworkers would laugh at that.

All of them really. Because technically, maybe she *was* taking care of people. Men. In the loosest sense of the words.

She shoved the lewd jokes aside.

That was something else. She'd had to get used to a whole new way of thinking. Just little things would bring the words and the images and the jokes and the things she used to laugh about and the things that used to make her angry to the surface.

"You don't look like a caretaker," the woman spat out. Again, it didn't sound like there was any kindness in her voice. "You look like a sultry tramp who's out to steal my husband."

Maybe a shadow passed over the woman's eyes at the word husband. Burgundy couldn't be sure.

"'Course the man's been dead nigh on five years now. Which is why I need a caretaker."

If her voice was a little bit less rough, less sharp, it was hard to tell. Still, whether it was the shadow, or whether it was the idea of being married for such a long time, and thinking of her loss, her words made Burgundy feel bad.

"I'm sorry to hear that," she said again.

"Don't be. It's over and done with. He's currently the better off of the two of us."

Burgundy looked the woman up and down, trying to figure out what she meant by that.

Maybe if she got the job, the information would come out.

She hadn't exactly put her best foot forward.

But, in her defense, her best foot had a turned ankle that was throbbing right now.

She took a breath and held her hand out with the best smile that she could muster. She was really good at smiling when she didn't feel like it.

"I'm Burgundy, and I'm pleased to meet you, Mrs....?" She figured the woman was Mrs. if her husband had died years ago.

The woman looked at her hand with suspicion, like she suspected Burgundy was holding it out as some kind of trick.

Her jaw worked before she finally stuck her old gnarled hand into Burgundy's. Her fingers were crooked, but her grip was surprisingly firm.

Burgundy didn't flinch, but she might have if it hadn't been a little old lady squeezing her fingers.

Thankfully, she wasn't wearing any of the rings that she might have been if she were back in her old life.

It'd been a full year.

In some ways, it felt like forever, and in some ways, it wasn't nearly long enough.

"You can call me Mrs. Scholz. That's what everyone else does."

The lady seemed to speak reluctantly, like she wasn't wanting to give up any personal information, or maybe she just didn't want to like Burgundy. Maybe it was a mixture of the two.

"It's such a pleasure to meet you, Mrs. Scholz. Pastor Race has highly recommended me. Here's the letter he wrote that he said I could deliver to you, to help you make up your mind."

Her fingers trembled ever so slightly as she pulled the note out of her purse and handed it to Mrs. Scholz.

Mrs. Scholz looked suspiciously at the paper and Burgundy's hand.

Everyone in Mistletoe had been super friendly to her. She'd even made a few dollars waitressing at the small coffee shop when the regular waitress spent two days visiting her mother.

She'd made a little more money selling Christmas trees for a couple of weeks before Christmas.

Both of those jobs had expiration dates though, and if she wanted to stay in a small town, which she did, she needed to find something that she could do that would pay enough for her to stay.

Maybe one time, her tastes ran to fancy. Not anymore.

Mrs. Scholz did not invite her in but stood in the doorway as she opened the letter and read down through it.

Burgundy had quit smoking, but she supposed the craving for a cigarette would never completely go away.

This was one of those times.

Not that she necessarily wanted the nicotine, she just wanted to have something to do with her hands.

She had been one of the lucky few who could do drugs without getting addicted to them. At least she never had. She supposed everyone had their tipping point.

It was only by the grace of God that she hadn't reached hers.

In her old life, it wasn't hard to see what drugs did to a person.

Mrs. Scholz seemed to be done reading the paper, but her head was still down, like she was thinking.

Behind her, there was a shout and a couple of dogs barking and what sounded like someone pounding.

Burgundy didn't turn to look. It was a farm, or something like that, and she supposed there were animals on it and people working. Made sense.

She also supposed that the animals wouldn't come up on the porch and try to get in the house, so she felt like she was safe standing there with her back toward everything.

"Well, might be against my better judgment, but I do have a tendency to trust what Pastor Race says." The woman's eyes were shrewd as she looked at Burgundy. "I'm gonna have to start you at half my regular rate, since you have no experience."

"You have a regular rate?" Burgundy had been under the impression that she was the first housekeeper that Mrs. Scholz had hired.

"I do." Mrs. Scholz named minimum wage.

Burgundy bit her tongue. Hard. The metallic taste of blood seeped into her mouth. Not unfamiliar.

She wasn't quite sure what Mrs. Scholz had suggested was legal.

Not that she was a stickler for being legal.

At least, she had never been before.

She'd changed. For the most part.

It was hard not to think of the money that she'd made in her previous profession.

Half of minimum wage wouldn't even pay for one minute.

But the work was wrong. And she was ashamed of it. And no matter how much she made, she wouldn't go back.

God, will I always be tempted?

She wasn't tempted because she loved her work; she could almost get to the point where she separated it as a job in her head. She didn't have to like what she was doing in order to do it.

She just did her best at her job.

Ugh. She was lying to herself, and she knew it. By the very virtue that it was her with her voice, her body, or both, it didn't matter. It was a job, yes, but it was a job she could have refused.

But she didn't.

"I suppose you can come in if you're accepting. You're not very talkative."

Too many memories.

"I'm sorry. I'll accept. How long is the probationary rate?"

"Two weeks," Mrs. Scholz said shortly. "If you're satisfactory, I'll raise it to minimum wage." She stepped back, and Burgundy stepped in. "We'll discuss it six months from then if we're both satisfied and talk about where we're going from there."

Mrs. Scholz might be a little lady, and kind of bent over, with gnarled fingers, but her mind was sharp as a tack anyway.

She walked in the house, which was cluttered to say the least.

Race hadn't given her all the details. He'd been called out to try to counsel a couple involved in the middle of a fight that involved breaking dishes and crying little children.

He'd given Burgundy the barest of details, handed her the letter, and told her he had to go.

"That sounds fine, Mrs. Scholz." Part of the job was that she would have a room in which to stay and food to eat.

She really didn't have ambition beyond that. Hiding out and putting her past behind her.

It would just take time.

She closed the rickety door behind her with a sigh. Knickknacks covered every surface. Burgundy tried hard to figure out a theme, but it seemed to be geese mixed with mushrooms mixed with pink flamingos maybe?

The rug she stood on sported a purple dinosaur.

Maybe the cohesive theme was that there was no cohesive theme.

Mrs. Scholz walked through a door on the right. "Obviously, this is the kitchen. I can cook. But the social worker that was in here said I should have supervision, which I completely disagree with, but in order to stay..." Her voice trailed off, and there was that shadow again.

Burgundy tried to set her past aside. Mrs. Scholz obviously had some pain in her past as well.

"You might as well know it now. I sold the farm. But," her eyes got crafty, "I made the sucker who bought it promise that I could stay here until I died. He insisted that I had to have a caretaker. So that's why you're here. He's afraid I'll burn the house down by leaving the oven on." The old lady shifted. "Maybe he's right. I have forgotten a time or two. But doesn't everyone?"

Burgundy nodded. "Actually, I have. I'm horrible at remembering to turn it off. I get involved in other things, and I've left it on all night before."

"Exactly! That's exactly what I told him. So normal."

Burgundy grinned and nodded.

Mrs. Scholz didn't exactly grin at her, but she felt like maybe they had a tenuous bond trying to form between them, united against whoever it was that had bought her house.

"So, there's someone else living here too?"

Those crafty old eyes shifted back, and the old lady nodded. "I can't believe Pastor Race didn't tell you that."

"He was kinda busy."

Which was fine. It didn't matter whether there was someone else living here or not. Although, she couldn't help the little tremolo of fear that gripped her heart every time she thought of meeting someone new.

Would they recognize her? Would they know who she was?

So far, she hadn't gotten the impression that anyone in Mistletoe knew. She'd really like to keep it that way.

Although, she kinda had a feeling that one's past had a tendency to catch up with one, and she doubted she was the exception to that rule. She hadn't been the exception to any others.

"Did you bring your stuff with you?" Mrs. Scholz tilted her head around as though looking for a bag would make one materialize near Burgundy.

"I have a couple of suitcases and a duffel out in my car."

It was everything she had in the world. When she'd hit rock bottom, she didn't have much left worth salvaging.

Most of the clothes she had were clothes that she'd gotten after she'd been rescued.

"Might as well go out and get them, bring them in here. We'll take them upstairs and show you to your room." Mrs. Scholz crossed her arms over her chest and stood back. Something about the discordance of her outfit made her blend right into the discordance of the house décor.

Funny how things seemed to suit each other.

Burgundy just hoped she found something that suited her.

As she walked out to her car, she saw a couple cows over by the barnyard, but no people.

Her heart wouldn't let her rest until she met the new owner of the farm and found out, by looking at his face, whether or not he knew her.

Her suitcase bounced along behind her as she limped back to the house. Her ankle wasn't twisted and would probably be fine, if a little stiff in the morning.

She walked up the porch steps a little more carefully this time.

She followed Mrs. Scholz upstairs, past piles of family pictures on the walls and shelves of knickknacks. She was careful not to bump them, even though she was a little off balance with her suitcases. That was not the kind of inauspicious beginning she wanted.

They took a right and went down to the far room. Mrs. Scholz opened the door.

"This is yours. It don't have too much stuff in it. It took me two weeks to clean this one out. Hope you're happy with it."

The bedroom was at the back of the house, with great big windows that stretched almost from the floor to the ceiling, giving her a gorgeous view of the backyard and what she assumed were pasture fields. She was more than happy.

The beauty outside more than beat the dingy window view of her apartment in LA. Even with the amount of money she made, she'd never had a great place to live.

Drugs were expensive.

"This is perfect. Thank you."

"Got some warm 'ems up we can have for supper. You can start cooking tomorrow." Mrs. Scholz started to back out the door. "We eat at six, whether that man is here or not."

Burgundy's eyebrows went up at that, but she didn't make a comment.

That man.

The way Mrs. Scholz spat that out made it sound like she didn't care for the guy.

"I'll be down early to help set the table."

She could earn her keep. But she did appreciate the chance to settle in.

As soon as the door closed, she went to her handbag and pulled out a ratty-looking gray stuffed elephant.

"Oh, Rosemary. Here we are. Another new spot. We probably can't put our roots down here, either. But maybe we can try putting out a few tentacles. We have to get the stuffy Mrs. Scholz to love us or at least like us a little."

She stroked down the soft gray fur and then squeezed the animal to her chest.

Rosemary had gone with her from move to move to move, although she hadn't gotten her until after the worst moment of her life.

She'd not been there when the first boy was in her bedroom at thirteen.

She'd not been there when she'd been voted "most popular" in her high school freshman class.

She'd not gone on overnight cheerleading trips.

And she'd not gone along on the senior class trip, when she shared a room—and a bed—with Todd and Brian.

"Why weren't you there to tell me that was wrong?" she asked Rosemary, holding the elephant away and looking into the one eye that was still attached. Most of the gray fur had been rubbed off. She looked lumpy and was probably filthy.

Burgundy would never give her up.

Rosemary didn't have to answer anyway. Burgundy might not have had moral teaching, and everybody had been telling her from the time she was little that it was okay as long as she used protection. Which she had.

But her heart had told her it was wrong.

Her conscience, her soul, her spirit. It never felt right. It might have been fun, and she'd always made sure she enjoyed herself.

But it never felt right.

Man, she wished she could go back and do it all over again. So much she'd do different

"We're starting over, Rosemary." She kissed the elephant and set her on the bed. Now, the room felt like hers.

Chapter Two

Crew climbed the steps to the house, avoiding the rotten board on the second step.

He needed to get that fixed.

There must be a storm coming though, because his hips hurt.

Funny, with the bends, he'd always heard it was the arm and shoulder joints that were affected.

His knees hurt some, but it was his hips that always gave him problems.

The doctor said it was probably just something he'd have to learn to live with.

A cane made it easier, but he couldn't stand being thirty-one and needing a cane. In another thirty years, maybe.

He put his hand on the door and took a breath. Steeling himself to face whoever was in there. He'd seen the car parked in front of the house. Pastor Race had told him he was sending someone to take care of Mrs. Scholz.

The finagling old lady had made it a condition of him buying her farm that she lived there until she died.

But she needed someone to take care of her.

Back in his younger days, Crew would have needed some alcohol to get him through this. Talking to women wasn't something he was ever good at.

Alcohol made it easier. A lot easier. Enough alcohol, and he completely lost his inhibitions.

He'd done a lot of things he was ashamed of, but that was all before he'd walked the aisle with his good buddy Denver.

Jesus had changed his life, but he still lived with the guilt.

He knew it was supposed to be gone, but he'd done some things that were hard to forget.

Still, he wasn't going back there, so he'd suffer through whoever Race had recommended to take care of Mrs. Scholz. Of course, in that same conversation, Race had also asked him if he would be a secret Santa for the town of Mistletoe this year.

If there was anyone who wasn't fit to be a secret Santa, it was him. But somehow, instead of the "no" that he intended to say, a "yes" fell out of his lips.

Pastor Race just seemed to have that way about him. Where he asked for things that were crazy and off the wall, things a man knew he should say no to but somehow found himself agreeing to them.

Look at Denver. He'd agreed to a marriage of convenience.

Kinda crazy how it had worked out. Denver had fallen in love, and his wife sure looked like she adored him. A happier couple Crew had never met.

Of course, he hadn't met too many happy couples in his life.

Throwing his shoulders back, he opened the door and walked in.

Well, he walked in his head. In reality, he was a little hunched over and stumbled like an old man. Limped? Shuffled? Gimped in, maybe. One of those was pretty much how he got around.

He shut the door behind him but immediately wanted to open it and walk right back out.

One look at the long blonde hair, narrow waist, and perfectly curved hips, and he knew he was in trouble.

He'd never be able to talk to her.

He'd faced plenty of scary situations in his life, where his life was in danger and the lives of the people around him were in his hands.

It never failed to baffle him why he could do that but to face a woman and actually get words to form was more than he could manage most days.

Why did you make me so weird?

Silence as always. God didn't usually answer his "why" questions.

He stepped into the kitchen to wash his hands at the sink, hating that he had to get up his nerve to walk into his own kitchen. This wasn't what he'd expected when he bought his own place.

The old lady was used to his silence and didn't greet him when he walked in. She did, however, give a sniff and slant her eyes at the caretaker before she turned back to the stove, stirring the soup she was heating on it.

The blonde turned, and her eyes widened a little before she started forward.

He wasn't sure what the eye widening meant.

Although, once she'd turned, she looked a little familiar.

He wouldn't know why she would; he could count on one hand the number of women he talked to for any length of time since he'd gotten sober.

Which meant, if he did know her, she was probably a woman from his past.

How that could be when he was from Galveston, Texas, and had done most of his carousing there, he would have no idea.

The woman had reached him, with a smile and her hand out.

"I'm Burgundy, and I'm the caretaker for Mrs. Scholz. I'm pleased to meet you."

Crew looked at the hand, which was white and perfectly shaped, smooth with shiny red nails. Matched her name. Matched the color of lipstick she wore.

Bracelets jangled on her wrist, and a necklace with a single cross hung around her neck.

He stared at the cross for a couple of seconds. Maybe she wasn't from his carousing days. Not if that cross meant what it was supposed to mean.

Sometimes, it didn't.

Sometimes, a person wearing it just couldn't live up to the standard it set.

He'd met women like that. Through an alcoholic glaze of course.

The silence had gotten awkward; he'd taken too long to respond.

Not that he was even thinking about responding. He wasn't going to be able to say anything.

"I believe Pastor Race said your name was Crew?" The woman's face had fallen just a little. The classic beauty marred by an emotion that could possibly be insecurity or maybe irritation.

That was a yes or no question he could jerk his head at. So he did.

Her brow shifted just a little, and the hand she was holding out moved slightly, like she was asking if he could respond to her but couldn't shake her hand?

He couldn't touch her. Couldn't talk to her either.

It was just one of the payments he had to make for being sober.

"Well, I guess I won't push myself on you," the woman said, brushing her hands down her sides, her cheeks pink, and her words coming out with embarrassment.

Awkward.

Which was the word that defined most of his dealings with women. Maybe, if he hadn't had the accident and were still whole, he would work on changing that.

He supposed the world would term it shyness. Shyness could be overcome.

But since he was never gonna look like anything except an old man, he didn't see the point. A cute little Christian like this girl wasn't going to look at him and see a potential partner anyway.

He turned abruptly and went to the sink.

※

BURGUNDY CLUTCHED Rosemary to her chest and crept silently down the dark creaking stairway.

It was one AM, and she just needed to get out.

Mrs. Scholz had turned out to be almost completely deaf without her hearing aids, but Burgundy didn't want to take any chances.

She moved quietly through the house, her heart aching, her stomach sick, her throat tight.

The wood deck boards froze her feet as she stepped out, closing the door almost completely but leaving a crack so she could get back in.

In LA, she'd cried on the fire escape at this time of night when she wasn't working and sometimes even when she was. She wasn't sure what it was that drove her, but she had to cry.

She sat down on the steps, welcoming the cold, feeling like she needed the uncomfortable pain almost as punishment. Punishment for the life she'd led, punishment for the things she'd done, punishment for not even feeling bad about stuff.

She hadn't felt bad. Not while she was doing it anyway. Most of the time anyway.

She definitely didn't feel bad about the men she'd used and left.

That had kind of been her thing—leaving men—starting at thirteen. She wasn't quite sure why. But she'd never wanted to stay with anyone. Once was enough, even that young. After that, she wasn't interested anymore.

She'd never considered, or cared, about any heartbreak.

She sobbed quietly, the tears rushing out, dripping down on Rosemary. She clutched the stuffed animal with her scruffy fur and faded colors. Rosemary had been the one thing that remained a constant in her life since she'd gotten her. The one thing that was always there for her.

Thankfully, five or so years ago, she'd had a housemate that had known how to sew, because at that point, Rosemary had been getting pretty ragged.

Clarisse had patched her up almost as good as new.

The thought of Clarisse made her sob harder. Clarisse had died on the same street that Burgundy had been rescued from.

Why did a person have to hit rock bottom in order to feel like they needed to be rescued?

She shoved a hand in her mouth to keep the noise that her agonized heart wanted to let out pushed down deep. The tears could come, but she couldn't wake anyone and couldn't let anyone know.

Why, Lord? Why did you save me and leave me with the memories?

If the sins are truly gone, God, why do I see every face?

It wasn't just faces she saw. There'd been a lot of bodies. People looked a lot different without their clothes on. She had those images burned in her brain.

Rosemary was wet with her tears, but Rosemary was used to it.

Burgundy had a feeling that if Pastor Race knew how truly, *truly* bad her past was, he wouldn't have set her up for this job and given her a recommendation.

She couldn't let anyone find out what she used to be.

Chapter Three

"No! Not that one. The other one. Grab the other one." Mrs. Scholz, her voice strong despite her diminutive stature, jabbed her finger as Burgundy stood on the ladder and pointed at the knickknacks on the shelf.

"This one?" she asked.

"You know what? Just take them all down. Get them all."

It'd been like that all morning. They had a huge bag of things to go out for donations. They had an even bigger bag of garbage.

Burgundy slipped the knickknacks into the bag. They were dusty. Mrs. Scholz was working on cleaning the things off before she put them in the donation bag.

"Are you sure?"

"I don't have any special feelings for them. All this junk around here was my sister's. She was the knickknack-y kind of person. I like things plain. With maybe a little flutter of a curtain at the window. And a nice picture or two. If I had a family, I'd put family pictures up."

"You were married? Did you never have children?" Burgundy made her words gentle as she slowly climbed down the ladder.

"Not really," Mrs. Scholz said, rather cryptically, Burgundy thought. How could one "not really" have children?

She supposed she knew a way, since she had two babies waiting on her in heaven.

It felt too much like prying to ask about that. Especially since she'd only been here a week.

Mrs. Scholz seemed happy with her work, and she had to say she enjoyed it, much to her surprise. She kinda liked trying to make a house into a home. With all of the clutter and junk on the walls, it felt overwhelming. As the clutter came down, it felt like the atmosphere in the home calmed.

She and Mrs. Scholz were going to be talking about wall colors soon.

The man who lived with them, Crew, hadn't said a word. Not a single one the entire week she'd been there.

Of course, she usually missed him at breakfast, since he was out before her, and she only saw him some at dinner. She had no idea where he went afterwards. Mrs. Scholz retired shortly after they were done eating in the evening, and Burgundy spent the rest of the day in her room usually.

Every once in a while, she got a little anxious to go somewhere. But normally, she was happy.

Although, today, they were headed to town shortly.

Not that there was much to do in Mistletoe. They were just going to get groceries.

"My bag's full. I'm coming down."

"That's fine. We'll leave it in the house, and we'll have that man take the shelf down. When we get the spackling, we'll have to patch those holes in the wall before we paint."

"Have you ever done that?" Burgundy asked, looking at her fingernails. That wasn't exactly in her skill set. She thought she could probably paint a wall.

Mrs. Scholz gave her a practical glance. Today, her shirt was purple and her pants were orange and black plaid. "Don't you young folks have YouTube? Look it up. We can do it."

Burgundy laughed. Mrs. Scholz wasn't nearly as bad as her bark would have one believe.

In fact, Burgundy actually had found Mrs. Scholz quite likable. In a rough-around-the-edges kind of way.

Burgundy herself was a little rough around the inside. She glanced down at her long fingernails again. Her edges looked good, although those nails would probably have to go. Just some things were easier to cover than they were to fix.

"Let's finish up here, then we'll head to town. You've been working hard all week, and I'll buy you lunch." Mrs. Scholz reached out for the bag Burgundy handed to her. "I'll finish cleaning these off, and then we'll have some things to take to the donation center in town." She shook her head. "Although who would want all this stuff, I have no idea."

"Maybe one or two pieces would be pretty," Burgundy said, hopefully diplomatically. She wasn't too much of a knickknack person. Rosemary was all she wanted.

Rosemary knew everything about her. She liked to think to herself that Rosemary loved her anyway.

Kind of like God, only without the judgment.

It was less than an hour later that they were seated at the Christmas Tree coffee shop in Mistletoe. True to its name, the Christmas Tree coffee shop had seven different Christmas trees in it.

Being that she was somewhat of a businessperson, Burgundy figured that the coffee shop could seat twice as many people if they took the Christmas trees out.

Since it was almost the middle of January, the Christmas trees were decorated with hearts for Valentine's Day.

Christmas music played from the speakers, and sparkly lights hung down from the ceiling.

Five years ago, she wouldn't have been caught dead in a cheesy place like this. But now, she kinda liked the atmosphere.

"There's the preacher's wife and her daughter. Looks like they're coming over. Be on your best behavior," Mrs. Scholz said under her breath.

Burgundy hid a grin. She supposed it was natural to act differently around the preacher and his wife, but they were sinners just like she was.

No. No one in this town was a sinner quite like she was.

Still, she couldn't see putting on a show, any more than what she already did, for any individual person.

"The preacher's wife doesn't determine whether we go to heaven or not. Why are we on our best behavior?"

"Because she'll go home and tell her husband, and Sunday morning, the sermon will be about you." Mrs. Scholz looked dead serious as she leaned across the table and whispered frantically.

Burgundy had to laugh. "I don't think Pastor Race takes his sermon notes from his wife."

"Think what you want. If my Ed wanted to be a preacher, he'd better take sermon notes from me. I could have straightened this whole town out." Her words were rough, but Mrs. Scholz softened them with a wink.

A wink that Burgundy might have missed a week ago. Today, she caught it and returned it.

"Burgundy! And Mrs. Scholz!" Miss Penny stepped over to their table. "It's so good to see you guys. How are things going out there? Are you two settling in?"

Penny just had that serene glow of someone who is perpetually happy. Someday, when Burgundy had a completely new life without the past that she dragged around like a ball and chain, she wanted to be just like Miss Penny.

"She's doing fair to middlin'. It'll take a few more weeks of training, maybe a couple months, and I'll have her whipped up into shape. She might make a half-decent helper." Again, while her words might have seemed harsh to Burgundy a week ago, now she just saw them as part of Mrs. Scholz's personality. Nothing less.

Miss Penny must have known how Mrs. Scholz was too, because she smiled. "That sounds really fabulous. I don't want to keep you guys, but I was wondering if I could talk to you for a second, Burgundy?"

Burgundy's head jerked up. She hadn't been expecting that.

"Um...I guess. Sure." She fumbled with her purse and slid awkwardly out of her seat.

"Oh, I'm sorry. I don't think I introduced my daughter, Journee? Maybe you've met her?"

Burgundy tried to give Journee a friendly look. Girls like Journee —fresh-faced and completely innocent—always made her nervous. Although she seemed like she was about the same age, and Burgundy would love to be friends. "I have. I saw her a couple of times when I was out working with Denver and Natalie selling Christmas trees."

She held her hand out for Journee, remembering her as a bubbly girl who always had a smile. The kind of girl who would never do what Burgundy had done.

"It's good to see you again."

Journee, her eyes dancing like life was a daring adventure, grinned and pumped her hand. "I've thought of you a lot. I hope we can do something together sometime."

"Yeah. We'll have to."

It was people like Journee who made her feel the most guilty. Having no clue how depraved people could be, she exuded happiness and a fixed determination that everything in her life was going to turn out right.

Burgundy didn't think she'd ever been that innocent and certainly never that sure that life was good.

She most definitely didn't have anything in common with Journee, even though they probably weren't too far apart in age, with Burgundy being almost thirty.

Journee began talking with Mrs. Scholz, sliding into Burgundy's seat as Burgundy stood.

"I don't want to take you or keep you for very long," Penny said, low and soft as she put her arm in Burgundy's arm and led her to the side of the diner, beside the Christmas tree whose Valentine's Day hearts were made out of colored macaroni.

"It's okay. What can I do for you?" Burgundy pushed her doubts aside. She knew her sins were forgiven. Even if God had had to put a little more effort into her sins than he did into most people's. Still, it was hard to remember and harder to act like she hadn't done what she did.

"My husband is starting a Secret Santa thing." Here, Penny tilted her head and put her hand up. "I know. I know. It's not Christmas. But we do live in Mistletoe, and we have things like the Christmas Tree coffee shop and the Holiday House, and our parking meters are in the shape of Christmas trees, and we keep our decorations up year-round. You know, all of those things that make Mistletoe unique and bring tourists in."

She'd paused for a second to smile a little. It was a little nerdy the way Mistletoe totally lived up to its name. And it had been getting worse over the last few years, since people had figured out that tourists would actually come to Mistletoe and want to see their Christmas spirit, even in March, July, September, and December. Everyone had kinda been getting into the game and spirit of things.

"Anyway, we have some families in the area that can use a little Christmas cheer, even in January. So, my husband has enlisted the help of Santa, but the Santa is kind of..." Here, Miss Penny bit her lip a little. "He just isn't as spry as he used to be."

Burgundy did not allow her lips to turn up. Miss Penny was trying to find a nice way to say the Santa was as old as dirt and couldn't do much more than say ho ho ho.

"Santa needs a helper to be his arms and legs and help spread some of that cheer we were hoping to spread through the town and surrounding areas. With the downturn in the economy, people can really use it."

This seemed like a good time to ask the question that had bothered her last Christmas—her first as a Christian. "But the church is about Jesus. Why are we using Santa Claus?"

That was something that had been kind of a pet peeve of hers since she started going to church a year ago. If Jesus was the reason for the season, they didn't need Santa.

"I don't want to take away from Christ in any way. Good point. But the idea that people can be as loving and giving as Jesus is, following his example, is a thing that can resonate with everyone. And since it's a little bit more acceptable to go around dressed in a Santa suit than dressed as Jesus, that's what we're going to do."

Okay. That explanation made a little bit of sense to her.

"We don't want people to think too much about who is doing the giving, but just be a blessing with no strings attached."

That made sense too.

She nodded while Miss Penny looked at her. That soul-searching kind of look that made it impossible to hide all the things she needed to. But she didn't feel judged. Although, she definitely didn't want what was in her soul to actually be available to Miss Penny's view. Miss Penny wouldn't be asking her to do anything at all if she knew the truth.

"Things seem to be going very well between you and Mrs. Scholz. I don't know that I've seen that lady smile but once in the last five years, and yet I think she smiled twice this morning already." Miss Penny grinned, in a teasing kind of way. Burgundy knew her words were meant to be light—a compliment—and not critical.

That's the way she took them. "I actually like her. I was a little scared at first, but she's a really nice lady with just a little bit of a hard shell."

She reminded Burgundy of herself.

"I think a lot of us have our hard shells," Miss Penny said, although Burgundy could hardly imagine her having a hard shell. "We have soft insides. We want to protect them." Miss Penny stumbled a little, like maybe she had her own soft inside she was protecting. Unbelievable. Then she shook her head. "Do you think you might be interested in being Santa's helper?"

"I'd love to."

Chapter Four

Crew took his cowboy hat off and stepped into the house.

He both dreaded and looked forward to this time of the day. For maybe an hour during supper and its cleanup, he spent time with Burgundy.

Not that she would know that he cared.

He hadn't been able to get himself to even say "hi."

He supposed it was real manly of him to admit that seeing her made him want to go over and touch her while, at the same time, he had an almost uncontrollable urge to hide under the table.

It did not, however, make him want to talk, not in the slightest.

Maybe that's why he'd turned to drugs and alcohol in the first place. It made life easier.

In some ways.

He looked around the walls of his house, noticing a difference. Whether that was Burgundy insisting that the shelves of clutter needed to come down, or whether Mrs. Scholz hadn't been strong enough to do it on her own, he wasn't sure.

Actually, he had a hard time imagining anyone making Mrs.

Scholz do anything she didn't want to. She must not be as spry as she insisted she was.

Still, he didn't miss the clutter.

Not that he spent much time in the house anyway.

Today had been a good day, and he felt like he was barely limping as he walked into the kitchen. Still, his stride was nothing like it was pre-accident.

"Good evening, Crew." Burgundy looked up from where she was stirring something on the stove. It smelled delicious.

That was all Mrs. Scholz. He'd seen the older lady giving Burgundy instructions. He had the feeling that she hadn't had the slightest idea of how to cook before she came.

She matched him in that area anyway.

He jerked his head. All the practicing that he'd done all afternoon to try to get up enough of whatever it took for him to push some words out of his mouth went flying out the window when her big brown eyes landed on him.

Man, he was an idiot.

He probably was not the first man to be an idiot.

Not over big brown eyes and long blonde hair and a figure that dipped and curved in all the right places.

He tore his eyes away and went to the sink.

There was a line shack down by the creek. It doubled as an old hunting cabin. He thought he could fix that up and stay there.

He didn't need a house. And it would be easier to be away from her, instead of being tortured every day.

"Go ahead and cut the tops of those green onions up. We can use them for garnish," Mrs. Scholz said. Burgundy stepped away from the pot on the stove and picked up the green onions.

The lady thought he was rude. He felt like he was, or there was something else wrong with him. It shouldn't be this hard to get his words out.

Maybe a little bit of alcohol would be a good idea. He just didn't know if he could drink a little without becoming an alcoholic all over again. There didn't seem to be a middle ground for him.

"I've got them, and I'll carry that pan over to the table in a minute. It's pretty heavy."

"I've been carrying heavy pans all my life," Mrs. Scholz said, but Crew noticed she didn't go pick up the pan.

Her words made Burgundy look up, then the knife snapped on the cutting board.

"Ouch!" She dropped the knife with a clatter and grabbed a hold of her finger.

She held it with her other hand, but not before Crew saw the blood dripping down. She'd really gotten herself good.

He took three steps to her, holding his hand out while reaching up with his other and opening the cupboard door where he stored his first-aid supplies when he moved in.

Her eyes, big and doe-like, but with sadness in their depths, sadness that he wished he could help with, looked up at him.

She couldn't know by looking at him, but he slept with his window cracked. His room was right above the back porch.

She couldn't know that he knew she was out there every night, crying.

He wished he knew why.

Her mouth moved, like she chewed on the inside of her lip, then her hand loosened. She lifted her other hand and placed it in his.

Even though he had his hand out, he hadn't been expecting her to give it to him, and his breath caught.

But he couldn't stand there and stare at her. She was bleeding. Still, it was hard to drag his eyes away.

He flexed his jaw and looked down at her hand, pressing the gauze he held against her wound to stop the flow of blood.

Giving the gauze a few seconds to sop up the blood, he lifted it gently. Just as he figured, not deep enough to need stitches, just deep enough to bleed a lot.

Mrs. Scholz had come over and stuck her head in.

"Girl. We don't want any finger in our salad."

Mrs. Scholz had a tough bark, but her sharp blue eyes were filled with concern and her brows were knotted as she looked up at Burgundy. "If someone didn't keep their knives so sharp, this wouldn't have happened."

Crew didn't say anything. Even if he could have spoken, there wasn't anything he could say to that. Mrs. Scholz wasn't really upset that his knives were sharp. She was just worried about Burgundy.

He pushed the gauze tighter on her finger and held it out, so she would take it and know to be putting pressure on it.

She did it without him saying anything, and he reached back up in the cupboard to find the container of bandages.

After taking two out, he removed the gauze and put a bandage on with enough pressure to help stop the bleeding. He covered it with another one.

"Isn't that a little tight?" she asked him, maybe a little hesitantly like she wasn't really expecting him to answer.

He removed his fingers from hers and picked up the bandage box, noticing his knuckles were white as he held it.

He could do this.

"Keep it on tight to be sure the bleeding stopped. You can make it looser in a few hours."

He put the bandages up in the cupboard, closing the door.

After washing his hands one more time, he pushed through behind Burgundy to reach the cutting board.

Burgundy stepped away, but her scent remained. Peppermint. And maybe a little vanilla. Funny how a scent could make a man long for things he couldn't have.

He needed to get that shack fixed up.

Taking up a clean knife, he picked up where Burgundy had left off cutting the green onions, having no idea what they were for, just that they needed to be done.

Mrs. Scholz bustled around the kitchen, as much as the older lady could bustle, insisting that Burgundy sit down, that she would take care of getting supper on the table.

When the older lady came over to the stove, beside where Crew was working, he put up a hand. He'd heard Burgundy tell her she'd set the heavy pot onto the table.

Now that she wasn't able, he would.

He made sure the knife stopped when he turned his face away from the onion though. He didn't want to end up like Burgundy. Although he was using a different knife, it was just as sharp.

Mrs. Scholz looked up into his eyes, maybe the second time she'd met his gaze since he moved in. He couldn't blame her for resenting him. This was her home, and she'd been forced to sell.

He hadn't had to agree to let her stay; he could have insisted that she go. She didn't exactly have buyers beating down her doors.

But for some reason, she took his inability to talk personally.

Except tonight, maybe because he'd helped Burgundy, Mrs. Scholz's glance was almost warm.

His voice, when he tried to use it, was rusty. "I'll get it."

He took the knife and pointed at the chopped-up onion on the cutting board before putting the knife in the sink and walking around Mrs. Scholz to get the pot.

He set it on the hot pads on the table, then forced his feet to walk to Burgundy.

He didn't really have to force them. It was more his feet walked to Burgundy, forcing his brain to go along with them.

He held his hand out, and she looked at it for a good ten seconds before her face lifted to his. There was almost something sensual in the way she looked at him before her gaze was quickly schooled.

That sensual look seemed familiar. And he had that feeling again. The feeling like he knew her. The one he got the first time he saw her.

He was almost sure he had seen her before.

But it was impossible. A sweet little church girl like Burgundy wouldn't have been anywhere near the places he'd been.

Her brows went up, like she was waiting. He almost rolled his eyes. She wanted him to talk again.

Man, she had no idea how hard it was. Why did he have such a hard time?

He'd never had a problem on the ship with all his buds. Never. In fact, sometimes he couldn't shut up.

He didn't know what it was about women, and most especially about Burgundy, that made him clam up tighter than the national vault.

But she wasn't budging, and he wanted to make sure the bleeding stopped.

His eyelids lowered slightly, and his voice was almost a growl. "Give me your hand."

If she even tried to make him say please, he was walking away.

Maybe she knew she'd gotten four more words than what he'd originally been going to give her, because she put her hand in his.

There was blood on the bandage, but it hadn't soaked through. If it was still bleeding, it was just a seep. She was gonna be okay.

He thought about telling her he wasn't going to be home that evening, thought about telling her he'd check it when he got back, except he didn't know when that was going to be, and he didn't have a voice to say that much anyway. So he just jerked his head down once, to let her know it was good, and then released her hand and went to sit down at his place.

Maybe he didn't want to go to the shack.

The tension was hard, and it was even harder to spit those words out, but it was a delicious tension that curled delightfully in his stomach and made him want more.

It was something he'd never felt while sober. He liked it.

Chapter Five

Burgundy had made sure that Mrs. Scholz had gotten to her room okay for the evening, and then she'd driven to Mistletoe, parking at the back of the church where she was supposed to meet the secret Santa.

She'd even been given a little elf costume, which was much more modest than any other elf costume she'd ever worn, but that part of her life was behind her now, and she had to stop thinking about it. She couldn't let it define her, choking her up with guilt and shame.

Good works didn't get her anywhere, but it felt like they did, and she was glad that Miss Penny had asked her to help.

When she pulled in, Santa was already there, standing beside a team of horses and a carriage.

Apparently in Arkansas, since there wasn't much snow, Santa rode in a carriage instead of a sled.

She kept from smirking, but barely.

She had to admit she was glad it wasn't cold enough for snow. She certainly didn't want any.

Her finger throbbed, but it didn't hurt anymore. The bleeding had stopped.

The thing that hadn't stopped was the tremble in her heart every time she thought of Crew touching her hand.

Goodness, if that's what the man could do when he said three sentences to her and put a bandage on her...good night, he'd be lethal if he were actually charming.

Good thing he wasn't.

She'd had enough of charming men. Although probably she'd been treated to the rougher side of humanity more than the average girl, too.

Charming was better than rough.

Real was better than either.

She had a feeling Crew was very real.

Whatever his hang-up was, he wasn't faking it.

He wasn't faking the concern that he felt for her either. Maybe that was where her heart got the tremble.

Santa was completely dressed in a suit. A big bushy beard almost completely hid his face, and eyeglasses that could only be called spectacles with their tiny lenses in wire frames perched on his nose.

Maybe the belly was real, maybe it was stuffed, she wasn't sure. Although he was the first Santa she'd ever seen that used a cane.

Hopefully, this would get her mind off Crew. He'd left after dinner. Of course, he hadn't said where he'd gone.

Normally at night, she went to her room and didn't pay any attention to him. He'd carry the dishes from dinner to the sink and then go do whatever it was that he usually went and did in the evening. Maybe to his room, maybe to the barn, maybe who else knew where. She wasn't supposed to care.

She was working on that.

Slamming her car door shut, she straightened her green elf uniform, fixed her ears to make sure they were at the proper angle on her head, tugged her hat down between them, dug deep to find her confidence, and strode over.

There were no cameras, and her elf suit stayed on.

This was for the good of the community, and she was with someone that Race obviously trusted, or he wouldn't be there.

Probably a nice old gentleman from the church.

"Good evening, Santa," she said with a smile.

"Good evening. Does the elf have a name?" His voice was smooth with just the smallest curl to his words that marked him from the south. Somewhere. It was a curl that felt good in her stomach.

"I sure do," she said. "It's Bunny."

She almost slapped her forehead.

Why had she done that? Bunny was dead. Gone. That was her stage name. The one that she'd used before she'd gotten out of that mess. The one that was on all of her videos.

Stupid.

But it was out, and there wasn't anything she could do about it. So she upped the wattage of her smile. "Does Santa have a name?"

"Santa. Isn't that right?"

She laughed. His voice was cultured but obviously the voice of an old man. She bet he was seventy if he was a day and probably older.

"I've never seen Santa with a cane before," she said, not meaning to be rude, but just making conversation.

Maybe she'd hit on a sensitive topic though, because he was just reaching down to pick up the first package to put it on the buggy, and he froze, like her words had bothered him.

She was opening her mouth to apologize when he said, "That makes me unique then, right?"

"Sure does." She walked over and stood beside him, reaching down to get the packages. "Here, let me get these. I sure hope you're driving, because I have absolutely no idea of how to handle horses."

"They're not that much different than reindeer," he said, with a glint in his eye. He picked up the packet he'd had his hand on, but he let her do the rest.

"What happened to your finger?" he asked.

"I cut it while I was making supper tonight. It bled a lot."

"Hard to get a bandage on with one hand."

"Yeah, the guy that lives with me put it on." She thought about how that sounded and struggled to find a way to explain. "I mean, we aren't living together, like you know, like, he's not my boyfriend or anything. I just, I'm a caretaker. And the lady that I take care of lives with him."

That wasn't much better.

"He's not her boyfriend either. We just all live together."

She just gave up. Why couldn't she talk tonight?

Santa didn't seem to notice. In fact, he seemed really nice. Easygoing and calm. She liked him. She had no idea who he was.

On Sunday when they went to church, she'd have a look around the congregation and see if she could see any one of the guys who were walking with canes to try to figure out which one was her Santa.

"I see." And honestly, it almost seemed like he did. She hadn't had too many good experiences with men in her life, but for some reason, she almost trusted this man. And that was really saying something, because she never trusted men.

And she barely even knew him.

She'd never met a man who hadn't lied to her. Usually about little things. Then the little things turned into big things, and most of the time, they'd use her too.

In her experience, men were typically out for what they could get from her. They weren't interested in too much else. Sometimes it was money, sometimes it was other things, but in all her life, she couldn't recall a time when a man had done something nice for her and not expected anything in return.

That was just the way the world worked.

Except, Pastor Race had been different.

He'd given her a recommendation and hadn't asked her to pay for it in any way.

For some reason, she didn't expect him to.

"Do you need a hand up?" Santa had walked around the buggy beside her and had his gloved hand out.

She hesitated. "I should have worn a pair of gloves. I never even thought about it. They didn't come with my outfit."

"I don't own any white gloves. These definitely came with the Santa suit. I kinda like them. I'm thinking they're not going to stay white though."

"I'd say you're probably right," she said with a laugh, placing her hand in his and liking the old-fashioned gesture.

His hand was stronger than she had expected for an older man. And it felt odd, almost like Crew's had felt earlier in the day, which was really strange.

It'd been almost a year since she'd even touched a man. Maybe this was her new normal?

That explanation didn't sound right, but she couldn't think of anything else that sounded good either and couldn't figure it mattered anyway.

She got herself up in the buggy and took her hand back. Maybe, if they did this again, she could remember to bring her own gloves, and she wouldn't have that problem.

"Thank you," she murmured as he started to walk around.

She felt like she was much higher than what she was expecting. The buggy moved as the horses switched their tails and stomped their feet.

It was cold enough for their breath to come out in cloudy puffs, and she watched as the horse in front of her tossed his head.

"You didn't hitch these up yourself, did you?" she asked. She didn't know anything about horses, and to be honest, she was a little afraid of being this close to them, of not being able to control them. She wouldn't be any help, but she felt like she should offer. A man as old as Santa was shouldn't be hitching horses up by himself.

"No. They're donated, just like the packages and our time."

"I see. I guess you know where we're going?"

"I sure do. I've talked to Pastor Race, and we're going out to deliver these to a single dad and his four little kids. It's not so much that they're hard up for money, it's more that they lost their mom at this time three years ago, and the dad always has a hard time. His name's Levi Tanner."

That description rang a bell. "I think I've seen them in church. His kids are the most adorable little things. Always so quiet and standing beside him."

"Yep. That's the guy."

He untied the horses and led the buggy out to the street before he walked around. Getting up seemed to be difficult for him, although with all of the beard and glasses covering his face, it was hard to recognize his expression. He didn't grunt or groan like she might have expected.

It was dark, but thankfully it wasn't the time of night that she normally cried, although she definitely didn't want to be out late. Santa seemed like a nice guy, but he did not need to be seeing that side of her. Not so early in their relationship anyway. Such as it was.

"So, you're new in the area? Where'd you come from?"

Just making conversation, funny how his question wasn't nearly as innocent as what it seemed. Or at least the answer wasn't innocent. But hey, she could say the truth and still not give anything away.

"Well, I grew up in Idaho..." She smiled the smile that showcased the dimple in her cheek and turned to face Santa. "Do you want the short version or the long version?" Pretty convinced he would say the short version. After all, he was a man, and men never wanted to hear her talk. They always wanted to be doing other things.

"You can give me the long version. If we walk the horses, it will be at least two hours out to Levi's."

Her mouth hung open a little bit. Well, she walked right into that one.

All right, now she had to figure out how to make this a long version without saying anything that would shock the old man into a heart attack and help him figure out what she used to be.

She'd like to be able to hide behind the Santa beard.

"Well, like I said, I grew up in Idaho. My dad was a deacon in the church and the principal of the high school. Good man." Her family had been upstanding. They would die if they knew what she'd become. She certainly didn't tell them what she had done, although they talked a few times a year.

"I guess I was considered kinda pretty, and I fancied myself an actress. Went to Hollywood. Thought I was going to be big."

And that was the honest truth.

"It didn't work out that way."

Santa nodded, like he was actually listening to her. She could hardly believe he was. He was a man after all.

But he was giving a good impression of it anyway.

"So, I did a lot of waitressing." That was true. She did. Then she found an easier, better, more lucrative way to work. And get paid for it. Plus, she was finally in front of a camera. It'd been really good money. At first.

Unfortunately, the industry that she'd landed in was even more fickle than mainstream Hollywood. Her shelf life had been two years. She'd drawn it out for three.

That was after waitressing for five years, going to auditions, talking to people who knew people who knew people. Being cast as the extra crowd and all those things young girls with big dreams did when they went to Hollywood but weren't quite what Hollywood really wanted.

Los Angeles had the most beautiful waitresses in the world.

"My one claim to fame is..." Goodness. She almost told him about the commercial she'd been in. Would he recognize her from that? The commercial had been made two years before she started her "other" career.

"Are you trying to think about it? Did you forget what commercial you made?" Santa asked, a little bit of teasing in his voice and a lot of compassion.

That drew her. "No. I just thought maybe you would recognize it. It was a door commercial. They were selling front doors. It was kind of catchy, and they needed my full figure and not just my head, which was more."

"More money?"

"Yeah."

Okay, the conversation officially made her uncomfortable.

"And after the commercial?"

Figures, Santa was the first man in her life who was actually listening to her, and she didn't want to tell him anything more. "Nothing else. Just a lot of dead-end jobs." Boy, was that the truth.

"How'd you end up in Mistletoe?"

She wanted to say, "what is this, the Inquisition?" but that wasn't nice. The old man was just making conversation.

"How'd you end up in Mistletoe?" There. She turned the tables. She could be a good listener too. Although, she hadn't always been. In fact, she couldn't really blame the men in her life for not being honest with her or for not listening.

She'd been extremely dishonest, and she'd never cared to hear anything that anybody had to say to her. Definitely not if they were trying to tell her what to do or think and especially if she didn't want to.

Even if it was some boy she was initiating, she didn't want to hear it. She always planned to walk away, and there was nothing anyone could ever do to stop her. None of them had been able to. Her heart was stone.

Except it wasn't. Not at night. After midnight, her heart was a ball of mush, and all she could do was cry.

"I grew up in Galveston and became an underwater welder. I did a dangerous job for a lot of years and finally decided I wanted to settle down. I had some friends in Mistletoe, and I decided to settle here. Can't say I've regretted it."

Interesting that his past was sufficiently vague as well.

"You skipped right over that wife and family," she said, with a little tease in her voice. Not flirt. She couldn't flirt with a seventy-year-old. That was just weird.

"Never had any."

That was sad for Santa.

"No Mrs. Claus?"

"Nope. No Mrs. Claus. No elves. Just wasn't in God's plan for my life, I guess."

Oh, it definitely wasn't in God's plan for her life either.

Santa didn't seem inclined to add to his background, such as it was, and she didn't want to talk about hers anymore.

"Where'd you learn to drive horses?"

If the subject change annoyed or threw him, he didn't let on. "I hung out with my buddy, and I learned some about animals from him. It's not hard. You just pick up the reins and tell them to go. And they go."

"You're kidding."

"Not really. This team is well trained. I think anyone could drive them."

Burgundy begged to differ on that, but she didn't argue.

Looking up, she admired the stars and the brightness of the night sky.

Like he could see into her mind, he said, "Pretty bright, aren't they?"

"They are." The steady clop-clop of the horses' hooves provided such a relaxing background noise as she was lulled by the rocking of the buggy. "They're not nearly this bright in LA. You can hardly see stars there."

"Out on the ocean, miles away from anything, they're so bright it's like you can touch them. You wouldn't believe how the sky is just filled with lights of various brightness. It's amazing and something that never gets old."

"I've never been on the ocean."

He was so easy to talk to. And there was no pressure. He was too old for her and was not interested in her in a physical way at all.

It gave her the confidence she needed to just be herself. She didn't have to have her sex symbol persona on. It was the lens through which she almost always related to men. Or the more recent super-good Christian persona. The one that she'd been trying to adopt since her conversion.

It wasn't the right way to interact with people, but she didn't have a natural way. Not since she was thirteen.

But with Santa, whoever he was, she felt her shield slipping away.

"You should make sure you do that. I guess, I feel like this part of the country's the most beautiful part in the world. I mean, the Ozarks are just so amazingly breathtaking. The waterfalls, and the seasons, and so much natural beauty, and we get to live right by them, in farm country. We can make a living off the land and still have the gorgeous scenery around us. With the mountains in the distance. They just call my soul. But the sea, it will always have a part of my heart."

"What about the North Pole, Santa?" He was an old man, and she wasn't flirting, but she was teasing him a little.

"I don't spend any more time there than what I have to." He turned toward her and winked. "That's just between you and me. We don't want that getting out."

She laughed, and the sound felt free and light in the evening air with the stars above and the horses in front of them and the smell of fresh air natural and perfect.

She couldn't remember feeling this easy and free ever in her life before. No pressure, no feeling like she had to act a part or that she needed alcohol to grease the social interactions or drugs to enhance her experience.

Everything just felt natural and right. Perfect.

"Don't take this wrong, Santa. I wish you were forty years younger."

Chapter Six

_C_rew froze.

He was pretty sure that Burgundy had just basically said if he were forty years younger, she would like him.

Forty years younger with no cane. If he were forty years younger, she'd expect the cane to be gone. She'd expect his body to be whole and young. She'd expect his past to be as pure as hers.

She'd be disappointed.

Still, the Santa suit had given him the shield he needed, and talking to her was easy. For the first time in his life, he didn't need alcohol or drugs in order to be able to talk to a girl.

He wasn't sure if a Santa suit was better than alcohol, but hey, he'd take it.

He found his voice. "I think there are groups of scientists who are working on time travel."

She laughed again.

Such a beautiful sound. That's what was missing on the ship at night. He had the slap of the waves against the deck, and the feel of the wind on his face, and the stars overhead, and sometimes the laughter of the crew, but he missed the sweetness of a woman beside him. Sweet innocence and the beauty she brought. The fun with a little buzz of excitement.

Yeah, that would definitely make settling down in the foothills of the Ozarks far, *far* better than ever going out and about again.

Except, if he took the Santa suit off, the easy comradery that stretched sweetly between them would disappear.

Plus, she'd look at him with revulsion and disgust, knowing the way he acted at home and the way he acted now. She wouldn't understand his need for a shield. He didn't really even understand it. Maybe it had something to do with his parents splitting and shuffling him back and forth between relatives who didn't really want him, but he couldn't remember a time when his shyness wasn't all-consuming.

He'd learned to interact with the men on the crew. He'd had to. But women? Never.

They rode in silence for a while. A couple of cars passed them, but they weren't on a busy road. It was an easy silence, and he found himself wishing the horses would walk slower.

Pretty soon, the lights of a small village appeared on the horizon.

"I think this is their lane." He squinted to see if he could read the green sign.

"That's one disadvantage the buggy has over a car. The car has lights at least."

"True. But I can make it out now, Land's End Lane. That's the one."

They turned down it, and she said, "Do you know what we're bringing them?"

"Miss Penny said Levi wasn't a good shopper, hated it, actually, so she picked out some clothes for the boys, which I'm sure they're not going to be very excited about."

He laughed to himself. What boy was ever excited about getting clothes?

He glanced over, because Burgundy hadn't said anything, and she was kind of looking at him in a confused way.

He took a wild guess. "You've never been around boys, have you?"

Her eyes widened, her mouth opened even farther, and she almost looked guilty. What did that mean?

She seemed to shake herself though, and the glint came back into her eyes. "No, not little boys. I don't have any brothers or anything."

She sounded a little breathless. That was odd.

"I don't think I've ever met a boy who was actually happy to get clothes. They'd much rather have toys. Or food. Preferably toys and food. If you can make food into a toy, that would be good."

"That doesn't sound very sanitary."

"If you're listing things in order of importance, sanitary would not make any boy's top one thousand list."

"Okay. I'll keep that in mind." She grunted. "Am I allowed to not like little boys very much?"

He had to laugh. "If you're going to be Santa's helper, you really have to treat boys and girls equally. I am an equal-opportunity toy giver."

"So I could lose my position if I favor girls over boys?"

"I don't know about that. We are kind of hard up for helpers... you'll be reprimanded. And your salary docked."

"Cool. This is a paid position?"

"Sure is. God will square up with you when you walk through the pearly gates."

He pulled into the parking area beside the car that was already there.

"Something else a car has over a buggy—there's no horn."

"I could yell?"

He looked over at her, wishing his glasses weren't on his nose. They kind of distorted the view, although she was still beautiful. Just a classic cut to her cheekbones and a perfectly shaped nose. Her jaw was squared and well-defined. Plus those doe-brown eyes.

"You must be quite a heartbreaker."

"Are you talking about my yelling ability?" She smirked. "You haven't heard me yet."

He hadn't meant to say that. Oops. She'd moved right past it, though, having no idea he'd actually meant it.

He could move on. "I just don't think a little thing like you can yell like we'll need. I think I'd better get down and knock on the door."

"I thought you needed a chimney."

"You want to put the Santa suit on? I'll find a chimney for you."

"Let's knock on the door."

"That's a good idea. I should have thought of that."

"You did."

"Yeah, but then you argued with me, and I had to offer to give up my Santa suit. What if the kids caught us exchanging clothes?"

"We might both get fired."

"I'm pretty sure we just decided there was no firing. We'd get reprimanded. Lose our salaries. Although, since there is no salary, we probably *could* get caught changing clothes. But it might not be good for the kids to see that."

"Good point." She seemed a little bemused and maybe a little smitten. As much as a young, sweet girl could be with an old man.

The idea didn't sit well, but it did give him confidence. Maybe she just needed him to be a little goofy to cheer her up.

He hooked a rope onto the horse's bridle and tied it loosely around the porch banister.

West's team was well trained, and he doubted they'd go anywhere, but he didn't want to take that chance.

He waited for Burgundy to come beside him, and they walked up the steps.

He knocked on the door.

Chapter Seven

Burgundy held the packages in her arms as Santa knocked on the door.

She'd been awfully curious about the identity of Santa, but the more she talked to him, the less she wanted to know. It just felt nice to be able to talk to someone and not worry about who they were or what they wanted from her. She felt, in the short time they'd spent together, that she could tell him anything. Like he was the father she'd had but never appreciated.

She'd never felt just right with anyone like that, ever, and couldn't believe it had taken less than a couple of hours for her to get to that point with Santa.

Everything just felt right when she was sitting beside him. Comfortable. Like she'd come home.

Santa lifted his hand to knock again, and she shifted the bags from one hand to the other.

Before his hand connected with the door, it got yanked open, and a young boy stood staring.

Burgundy had no idea how old he was. Five? Seven? She'd never really been around kids.

Anyway, he'd yanked the door open so fast it slammed against the wall, rattling the glass in the window and startling Burgundy. She cringed.

Santa didn't seem fazed. Funny, that, since he'd claimed to have never had kids.

She thought about teasing him about it on the ride home, but maybe he'd ask about her kids.

That was a subject she didn't want to get into.

The kid rubbed his eyes. Blinked. Rubbed his eyes again. His nose scrunched up. "Santa?" His eyes shifted to Burgundy, and she tried for a smile, which the young boy ignored. His eyes shifted back to Santa. "Are you lost?"

"Ho ho ho," Santa said, causing Burgundy's head to snap around.

He actually sounded authentic. She wanted to tell him so, but then she remembered she was supposed to be an elf and supposedly she heard that all the time.

She snapped her mouth closed and turned her head back to the boy.

"Is this the Tanner residence?" Santa said, in a jovial tone that was at odds with the more serious and adult tones he'd used on the ride there. Whoever was acting out the Santa thing, they were doing a great job. She'd have to ask on the way home if he had experience.

"Huh?" The kid's face scrunched up again, with his brows lowering. He looked over his shoulder and screamed at the top of his lungs, "Is this the Tanner home?" And then, almost as an afterthought, he screamed in the same tone, "Santa wants to know."

Burgundy bit back a huge smile. The kid was adorable.

There was some running and thumping and a couple shouts from upstairs, but no answer to the kid's question was forthcoming.

"I'll have to get back to you on that," the kid said, then he slammed the door shut.

Burgundy stood in stunned silence for about three seconds.

Santa must have been just as shocked as she was, because he was staring at the door too.

Finally, she heard puffs of air. They had to be chuckles. She turned her head to see.

There, in his beard, she saw a flash of teeth.

"Well, that's the first time that's ever happened to me."

"You've knocked on a lot of doors wearing a Santa suit before?"

"First time."

They laughed.

"You do the Santa thing really well. Those ho ho hos sounded like a real Santa. Straight out of a movie."

"Pretty sure in the movies, the kids don't slam the doors in Santa's face. And here I thought I might get mobbed. I'm not sure which is worse."

"I think getting mobbed." Burgundy was pretty sure that was true. Getting the door slammed hadn't hurt a thing.

"Maybe all the brothers are younger. I think I could take them."

Burgundy looked the old man up and down. He leaned on his cane with one hand on top of the other, hunching over it. She thought maybe her estimate of seventy might have been a little young.

"I hate to break it to you, Santa, but at your age, maybe you should leave the wrestling to the younger folk."

The flash of teeth was gone, and she felt like she'd said something wrong, although she had no idea what it was.

Did old men not like to be reminded that they were old?

She knew women were always lying about their age. Either to make themselves older or to make themselves younger, but in her experience, usually men didn't. Of course, her knowledge of the world was somewhat skewed.

She was trying to rectify that and put her dirty past behind her.

It made sense that maybe no one liked to be reminded they were growing old.

"I'm sorry. I didn't mean to rub your age in."

Santa was staring at the door, and he didn't turn his head when he said, "It's okay," in a tone that made it sound like it really wasn't okay.

For as much time as she'd spent with men, for as close as she'd gotten to him, she had no clue what to do.

Of course, she knew men's bodies. That's what she knew. She didn't really know their hearts.

She'd always thought of them as kind of simple and slightly stupid, with most having no idea of how to handle a woman.

In fact, most of the men she'd been around had been, honestly, rather easy to manipulate. Suggestive looks, some bare skin, and a man would do whatever she wanted.

Maybe there were other kinds of men in the world.

Men that had a heart. Or conscience. Or both. Feelings, even.

She opened her mouth to say something, but the door opened again. This time, a man stood in the doorway.

"By Job, you're right, Grant. It is Santa," the man murmured, obvious disbelief in his tone. His eyes swept to Burgundy, then back to Santa. "Are you lost?"

This time, Burgundy couldn't contain her snort. Very un-elf-like.

"Ho ho ho, Merry Christmas. If this is the Tanner home, I'm right where I'm supposed to be," Santa said.

"I'm Levi Tanner, so you're at the right spot. But I don't understand."

"You don't have to understand, you just have to listen. Or we can leave the gifts right here on the porch."

"No, you don't have to do that. I'm sorry. I guess I've been rude. Come on in." The man opened the door wider and stepped back. Santa, ever courteous, allowed Burgundy to go first with an outstretched hand.

"Thank you," she said, trying not to feel bad that she'd not made things right between them.

One more thing she wanted to talk about on the way home. She would give him an apology. A sincere one.

The house was happy chaos. Toys lay scattered everywhere, a TV blared from somewhere, with the occasional thump and bump and yell.

It was a house that looked lived in. Happily so.

"Sorry about the mess. It's hard to keep up with everything," Levi muttered as he closed the door behind them and gestured to the couch. "You guys can sit down if you want."

"If you don't mind, we will. Just for a few minutes though," Santa said, watching as Levi swiped a bulldozer, three blocks, and a dirty sock off the couch.

"I need to run back out and grab the rest of the gifts," Burgundy said. Setting the sack that she carried down, she walked toward the door.

Santa had stopped in the act of moving toward the couch. She got the feeling that he wanted to offer to help but couldn't.

She hadn't thought about what that might be like, to want to do something with your body as simple as walking outside and carrying a few things in and not being able to. Must be awful to get old.

"How many are there? Do you need my help?" Levi asked as his kids gathered around, staring at Santa.

"If you don't mind, please," Burgundy said. If he helped her, she'd only have to make one trip.

Again, she felt like Santa didn't approve. But he didn't say anything, shuffling the rest of the way to the couch and sitting down.

Levi opened the door for her, and she couldn't help noticing he was tall with broad shoulders and had a rancher's hands. Not the kind she was used to seeing in LA, but a real man's hands—a real working man's hands.

He was the kind of man that a girl would notice no matter who she was. He definitely commanded attention, although he seemed a little overwhelmed with the children.

"It must be hard with your wife gone."

"I guess. She was gone a long time before she actually left. If you know what I mean."

"I do." Oh boy, did she ever. She'd never been the other woman, thankfully. She wouldn't want to have a broken marriage on her resume, although she supposed with her movies and the things she'd done, she probably had caused the breakup of more than one marriage.

The thought didn't sit well. It never had.

"So what is this all about anyway?" Levi reached the back of the buggy with her and started stacking gifts in his arms.

"From what I understand, at the church they wanted to have more Christmassy activities to go along with the Mistletoe name of the town. They wanted to bring some things to your children because they knew that you didn't have a wife who was here to go shopping and pick clothes out and usually men don't like to shop. I understand the boys probably aren't going to be super excited about most of their gifts. Although from what I've heard, they threw a few toys and fun things in too."

"Oh, I see. So it's not a charity thing." He sounded happier than he had before.

"No. I think it's just to encourage you and to help out where they thought they might be able to. I believe Miss Penny is the one who did the shopping, and she's got an eye for sizes."

"She also has an eye for someone who hates to shop. I'll have to tell her I appreciate it."

"I'm sure she would like that."

They gathered the last of the packages up and started back toward the porch.

"Looks like you guys did it right, with the buggy and horses and everything. I guess Arkansas is a little too warm for reindeer?"

"It is." She laughed. "I had the same thought. It's actually kind of nice to ride in the buggy. Maybe a little bit cold."

"You have to snuggle up to Santa," Levi said, bounding up the stairs and grabbing the door in front of her, holding it for her.

"I don't think we have that kind of relationship," she said a little awkwardly. It was an innocent remark, and she should have just left it, but even innocent comments could take on a suggestive tone with her background.

Would she ever be normal?

"Thank you," she said as she walked through the door.

She almost fumbled to a stop. Santa sat on the couch, but she could hardly see him.

Four little boys had climbed on top of him, one on each leg, a little one standing on the couch beside him and leaning into him, and another one standing between his feet and trying to squeeze between his brothers.

All four were talking at one time.

"Boys," Levi said.

No one listened. Burgundy wanted to suggest to him that they probably couldn't hear him, but she figured children was one of the many areas where she had absolutely zero experience, and she shouldn't be telling anybody what to do with theirs. So she stood mute beside him. She had to smile at Santa being mobbed.

He'd said he could handle it.

She supposed she would have to tease him a little about that since he'd actually gotten the chance to "handle it."

He seemed to be holding out okay, too. At least, he wasn't screaming for mercy.

"Boys!" This time, there was no missing the authoritative ring in Levi's voice, although he hadn't raised it but a notch or two.

The noise stopped immediately.

"Let Santa breathe." He muttered under his breath, "We'll definitely make national news headlines if my boys managed to kill Santa tonight."

"Shouldn't be too bad. We have plenty of time until Christmas to find another one." Santa's head jerked up at that. She wished the beard were gone so she could see his face. She continued, "If he were Cupid, it might be a different story."

Burgundy smirked. Valentine's Day was only a few weeks away.

"If I were Cupid, I'd have a lot less clothes on," Santa muttered, causing the boys on his lap to look at him quizzically.

Burgundy snorted, meeting Santa's eyes across the room. She liked a man that could make her laugh. And his humor felt right. Like they got each other.

Levi looked between the two of them, like he was trying to figure out who they were.

It probably wouldn't be hard to figure her out, since she didn't have the advantage of a beard. But if he figured Santa out, she'd like to know.

"I'd offer you milk and cookies, but I'm fresh out," Levi said, coming around and grabbing the youngest little ones off the couch, lifting them easily and holding them on his sides. It was a natural gesture that was so unusual to Burgundy's eyes that she couldn't help but stare. A man who handled a child like it was a natural thing to do.

Maybe this was the way men were in middle America.

She knew it was. She'd grown up in Idaho. This was the way the men were there.

When she'd gone to the West Coast, she thought the men there were hip and cool and knew things the men that she'd grown up with didn't.

And they did, to some extent, know things the men she'd grown up with didn't. But the things those men knew weren't the things that really mattered.

Things like holding a baby in their arms as naturally as breathing. Respecting a woman and holding the door for her. Talking to her like she was a human and not an object. Actually thinking of someone beside themselves and being able to carry on a conversation, with interest, about things that didn't directly affect him.

Being able to say one word to his children and have them quiet down and listen to him.

Being able to live in happy chaos, where toys were strewn about the floor, not dirty dirt, but a lived-in house look. A look that clearly said this house was a home and not a place where someone slept off their drug-induced high and hung out until it was late enough for them to go out again the next day.

A house like Crew's. Only Crew didn't have children.

Or a wife.

Maybe his wife had left him too. Not that she'd ever find out, since Crew would hardly be telling her.

"All right, I think the gifts are in the bags, and they're clearly marked with everybody's names on them. Let's dig in." Santa spoke with authority like he did this every day.

Burgundy grinned and reached for a bag, sticking her hand in and pulling out a package. As the two boys on Santa's knees settled themselves, his arms went around them, almost as naturally as their father's had gone around the little ones.

For some reason, maybe it was the way he adjusted himself, but Crew came to Burgundy's mind again.

He'd look good with little ones on his lap.

Chapter Eight

Crew held the reins of the horses loosely in his hands. His elbows rested on his knees, and he stared straight ahead. It wasn't exactly a Santa Claus position, but it made his hips feel a little better anyway.

The happy chaos in that home had been appealing in a way he hadn't even realized would speak to him.

He never really thought about kids too much, and families.

Hadn't had one of his own.

And that one didn't even have a mom.

Somehow, Levi had created an atmosphere where his children listened but still had a good time, and even though there was a lingering sadness from the missing adult, there was a happy, homelike feeling that just felt right.

He tried to glance unobtrusively beside him.

Or maybe, he simply had that feeling when he was with Burgundy. Odd.

He'd never felt that relaxed and comfortable, like the person he was with made him better, with anyone else before.

"You must have had children of your own. You're really good with them." Burgundy's voice came from beside him. It was funny how her voice sounded right too.

It wasn't too shrill or sickly sweet. It just settled on his ears with a feather-soft belonging that he could get used to. Except, he couldn't. She thought he was an old man.

Remembering to keep his voice old-man sounding when he answered, he said, "I told you. No wife. No kids. Never really thought about it."

"That's kinda me." Her voice sounded soft and thoughtful, although he didn't look at her. Didn't really want to be talking about kids with Burgundy. She should have them with some nice guy. A Sunday school boy to go with the Sunday school girl.

"They seemed messy and a lot of work. And like they'd take me away from the person that I really wanted to be paying attention to, which was me." She said the last bit with a little hint of humor in her voice, like she was making fun of herself.

"I think we're all that way? We want to pay the most attention to the most important person in the room, which is ourselves. Pretty fixated on getting ourselves exactly what we want, and you're right, kids do get in the way of that."

"Then, before you know it, the years have gone by."

He supposed he should pick up on that, since he was supposed be an old man whose time for having children had gone past.

Maybe his time for having children had indeed passed, but he wasn't an old man. Far from it. No matter what he looked like or how he felt.

Plus, he couldn't resist asking, "What are you talking about? You're not old. You have plenty of time left to get married, have a family, build a home with some lucky guy."

He couldn't keep himself from saying "lucky." It was telling, but hopefully she wouldn't take anything from it other than he was an old man who thought she was sweet.

"I guess I just don't think I could be a very good example to children."

He straightened, wanting to be able to see her.

The horses plodded along, the night was dark, but the sliver of moon provided enough light to see her fingers, twisting and knotting in her lap.

She'd struck him as a Sunday school girl, but apparently she'd done something she felt bad about.

"I guess that's the thing about religion, isn't it? The thing that everyone hates about it. It makes us feel guilty."

"I thought it was supposed to take your guilt away?"

"Jesus does that. Religion makes you feel guilty."

She was quiet for a moment. "Okay. You're right."

"I think guilt has a place."

"That's an interesting opinion. I haven't gone to too many counseling sessions, but the general consensus, I think, is that guilt is bad."

"I think it is, for the rest of the world. Like why should you feel guilty? It just holds you back. It's people trying to make you feel bad about yourself so you don't open up and be free like you should be. Or something like that."

"You say that like you don't agree?"

"I don't."

She waited a little, her fingers still clutching each other but no longer twisting.

"So what's your opinion?" she finally asked.

He considered for a while. People didn't really agree with him; his opinion wasn't a popular one. He twisted it over in his head, wondering how he could get it out without sounding so far-fetched that no one would believe it.

The idea worked for him. Kind of.

"I guess I feel like guilt is kind of like pain."

She snorted. "Really? Pain? In what way?"

He rubbed the reins with his thumb, running the pad of it down the soft leather, grateful to West for having his horses trained so well. He didn't know what he'd do if he actually had to drive the buggy and handle the horses.

He'd gone out to West's ranch one time to make sure he was able to drive. This was his second time holding the reins.

"I guess guilt makes us so that we don't do the stupid things that we did again. Or to keep us from doing worse things. Kind of the way you cut your finger, and you're more careful the next time. Because you know it's gonna hurt."

She seemed to think about that for a while, sitting quietly beside him, her hands still.

A little breeze ruffled across the fields, blowing by them, and he smelled the peppermint smell that he associated with her. The one that had just enough hint of vanilla to take the sharpness away and make it feel smooth and rich and soft in his soul. It was definitely a smell that he could come home to. Wanted to come home to.

He shook that feeling aside. Sure, she was living in his home, but it wasn't a permanent thing. She wasn't going to be his.

"I guess I can see that. I had never thought of it like that before. Where we do something wrong, and we say our conscience bothers us. It's almost a natural thing. Until we sear it, and then it doesn't bother us anymore, and we convince ourselves that what we're doing isn't wrong, and we convince ourselves what we're doing isn't hurting anyone, and we're just having fun and we're just making ourselves happy, but in reality, everything we do affects everyone around us and even people we don't know. So guilt doesn't just protect us, it protects other people too."

"Exactly. I hadn't taken it that far, but you're right. If I steal something, I feel guilty about it. But it didn't just hurt me, it hurts the store clerk and the other customers who have to pay more for things since it's the clerk that lost money on what I took. Guilt is a good thing in a society. And we're trying to tell ourselves we shouldn't feel it."

"But there does come a time when it's crippling."

She was right. Some of the things he'd done in his past, maybe they'd become crippling guilt.

"Maybe that's why the idea of having your sins washed away is so appealing. The guilt is washed away with them."

"Is it?"

"Should be."

"I wish I knew how. I wish I knew what to do to get rid of it. Because, while you're right, I think guilt is a good thing when you've done something and it makes you want to change and do right, once you have changed, you want to take that guilt away, so you don't have to live with that every day of your life."

"Well, at least the good thing about that is it will keep you from going back and doing what you had done again. It's like the pain I talked about earlier."

"Still, living with the guilt is hard. Crippling. It hurts."

Was that why she cried at night? This question almost popped out of his mouth. But he didn't want her to know he knew. After all, he was Santa. Santa couldn't know.

Maybe he should admit who he was. The problem was the Santa suit loosened his tongue. Just having that shield of protection around him, so she didn't know who he was, had made it so that he could talk with almost natural ease. He didn't want to take that away.

Once the Santa suit protection was gone, he might clam up again.

But he could work on it at home now that the ice had been broken, now that he had had a crack in his inabilities; maybe he'd be able to talk to her eventually without the suit. He was going to put every effort he could into it, because he really wanted to be able to come to her as himself.

Eventually, maybe be able to ask why she cried at night.

Find out about the little stuffed animal she held.

"I think the idea that God is big, that it was our God who created all this—" He put his hand up and swept it around, indicating the mountains shadowed and dark in the distance, the stars above them, bright and numberless, and the rolling hills of pasture and farm that they plodded through. Indicating it all.

"—and so much more." He thought about the sea and the endless stretches. How he'd stare at the surface of the water and think about everything that swam underneath. How much volume there was, how many different creatures, some they might not even know about. How much studying had been done on the ocean? Not nearly enough to cover its immensity. So much more than they could even imagine, and God had made it all.

"The idea of that big of a God loving us, and forgiving us, and saying that whatever sin we had done is gone. That he remembers it no more. That, in itself, is enough to take our guilt away." He was sure about that much, at least.

"But it makes me see how insignificant I am and how badly I want to work for him rather than myself." Her voice wasn't nearly as confident as his.

"I think that's what the intention is. I think that's why we're here, isn't it?" He indicated their Santa and elf suits and their position on the buggy.

"I guess you're right." She nodded thoughtfully and said softer, "I guess you're right."

Figured he was. It was what the Bible said. That would never be wrong.

"But I guess it doesn't explain why you don't want children. Not that I'm prying."

Of course he was. He was most definitely prying. He wanted to know what she had done, what she thought was so awful that would keep her from having children.

She was quiet so long he didn't think she was going to answer. And he supposed he really didn't mind. Just plodding along with her was nice. The clopping of the horses' hooves and the easy night breeze, even if it was a little bit chilly, wrapped around their silence and made it feel cozy. He was okay with that.

"I don't think you'd understand."

"I suppose you could be right. There's a lot of things I don't understand." There was a little disappointment in his voice. He'd thought she was going to tell him. Had been counting on it.

"Plus, I'm not here to get married and have kids."

That didn't really surprise him. It seemed like more and more women were uninterested in family and kids. It did, however, surprise him that he was so disappointed.

"I'm too old, but that's not your problem. Maybe you can't find the right man?"

"That's funny. I'm living with a single man. Not," she slanted her eyes over at him, with a sort of guilty look, but sincere as well, "like you think. I tried to explain earlier and made a mess of it. I'm a caretaker for Mrs. Scholz. Maybe you know her?"

He nodded his head and reached up and adjusted his Santa hat, making sure that his face was completely covered by his beard and glasses.

"Well, I'm living with her. And Crew. He's single."

"There you go. Maybe the Lord has it all planned for you. Kids and husband after all."

He didn't think it boded well for him when she laughed out loud, the sound sweet and light, although slightly derisive on the evening air.

"Crew hates me." She laughed a little more. "No. There's definitely no marriage and children in our future. Maybe he has brothers. I wouldn't know."

He had to remind himself not to give out information about Crew. He didn't want her questioning how well or even how he knew him. Talk about a quagmire.

"How do you know he hates you? Has he been mean to you?" What in the world had given her that idea? He'd never even really talked to her.

"He never talks to me. It's like all he can do to say hi. He hates me so bad he can barely look at me."

What she'd said was so shocking he couldn't think of an answer. In fact, he wasn't even thinking about thinking of an answer. He was just rolling it over and over in his head.

He was too shy to talk to her, and she had no idea. She thought he hated her.

The shyness that he'd fought all his life, the one that alcohol and drugs eased and made him able to interact with people on a regular —and what he thought normal—basis, had made her think he hated her. He'd had no idea.

He supposed he could stash some beer in the barn. Just have enough to loosen him up a little before he came in.

But he didn't want to go through that again. He'd fought too hard to be sober. He didn't want to risk losing everything he'd worked for. Even if he didn't know how he was going to keep his farm. He didn't want to lose it to alcohol.

"Are you sure that's why he doesn't talk to you?"

"I have no idea why else. He doesn't like Mrs. Scholz either. But I think the feelings are mutual there. She doesn't have anything nice to say about him. Just that he's rough and mean."

"Is he a harsh landlord?" Crew had to admit his heart was hurting a little. He hadn't realized Mrs. Scholz didn't like him, either.

Burgundy shook her head. "I don't think so. I guess, just because he doesn't talk to her either, maybe she got the idea that he doesn't like her, so she doesn't like him in return?"

That made sense. People did that all the time. Instead of treating people the way they wanted to be treated, they treated people the way people treated them. Even Christians. Despite the golden rule, which everyone knew. Christians quoted it, Christians knew it, Christians even had it memorized.

No one lived it.

Really, no one was encouraged to live it. If you were nice to people who were unkind to you, you were considered a doormat and a pushover and told you should stand up for yourself.

It was preached all over, even in Christian circles.

No matter that it went directly against Jesus's teaching.

But maybe, Crew figured, he wasn't living it either.

"Maybe he's shy."

She snorted. "Have you seen him? He's scary looking. I mean, he does kind of walk a little bit like you, but he's bigger, I think, and he's scowling all the time, and like he just has those broad shoulders and those muscles and everything that just tells you that he's strong and could break you in pieces, and he'll do it in a heartbeat if you cross him. That's the kind of guy he is. Not shy."

Okay. Well, she wasn't a very good judge of men.

But the whole golden rule thing had gotten him thinking. He wasn't really treating people the way he wanted to be treated. He was treating people in a way that made him comfortable. Not talking was more comfortable than talking for him, so...he didn't talk.

How would he like it if he'd been sitting there on the buggy seat, trying to talk to Burgundy, and she discounted him, and growled, and looked the other way?

He would have assumed she didn't like him either.

He wouldn't have assumed she was shy.

Something to think about.

Something to work on, actually, because his shyness, he could see clearly now, was actually him caring more about himself than about other people.

Interesting. It felt like an epiphany. Maybe somebody else had already figured that out and wrote books and books about it and he was just slow, since it wasn't something he'd ever considered before.

It was his personality, and he lived with it.

He never thought he'd have to overcome it.

But if he wanted to follow Jesus's teaching, like he had just been complaining in his head that no one else was following, then maybe he should actually do to others...what he wanted them...to do to him. Radical.

Radical when he thought about it that way.

"Just because someone looks scary doesn't mean they are," he finally said. Because he didn't know what else to say.

"Well, I can guarantee you that Crew both looks scary and is scary. And I'm not easily cowed."

"And that has what to do with the things you feel guilty about?"

He wasn't sure where that question came from, but he could almost feel the connection.

He hadn't meant for his words to dig up painful thoughts, but she flinched, like he'd struck her, which maybe he had with his words.

"I don't think I want to talk about that."

"I'm sorry. I didn't mean to push where I wasn't welcome."

"It's not that you're not welcome. It's just there are a lot of things about me that are ugly."

The lights of Mistletoe had come into view. There weren't many, but they were welcome. He hated for their ride to end on such a bad note. One where he'd made her feel bad.

"So, do you think we're going to be doing this again together?"

She turned to look at him. Maybe she was going to give him a tongue-lashing and a "you need to stay in your own business, then maybe I'll be happy to do this with you again" lecture. But she didn't.

She smiled, and it felt right in his heart. Putting a little glimpse of brightness into the corners that hadn't felt any brightness in a really long time, if ever.

"I hope so. You gave me some things to think about, and I love talking to people like that."

Oh yeah, the light just got brighter. Her smile, then her words, and it was enough to make his heart happy and warm him from the inside out.

He looked forward to their next ride together.

Chapter Nine

Burgundy seemed to spend all of her time on ladders lately.

Not that she minded, since it was helping to get rid of all of the clutter. Maybe not all, but most of it.

This time, though, she was super high, at the top of the cathedral ceiling. She'd be scared out of her wits, except Mrs. Scholz had stopped Crew, apparently, before he left after breakfast this morning and asked him to come in and give them a hand with the ladder later on.

Surprisingly, Crew had showed up.

Something Burgundy hadn't ever gotten over from her previous life was sleeping in.

Since she'd been here, Mrs. Scholz had been okay for breakfast. As long as Burgundy knew she was coming down a little later to check the skillet and the stove and the oven, she didn't get too worried about it.

So, Mrs. Scholz and Crew usually had breakfast together at some ungodly hour in the morning, and she came down at a much more reasonable eleven o'clock.

In her defense, she worked her butt off from then until nine or so at night. Once Mrs. Scholz retired for the evening, she tidied up, made sure everything was off, and did some light housekeeping into the evening hours. She was definitely putting her time in. Her hours just didn't start as early in the morning.

She really didn't see anything wrong with that. The best time to sleep was from about seven AM on.

Anyway, the ladder felt very sturdy with Crew down at the bottom holding onto it.

Even if he did walk hunched over, like an old man, and the more she was around him, the more curious she got about why he did that, she felt safe and secure while he was anchoring the ladder.

Maybe it was an illusion, but he gave her confidence. She stood on the second rung from the top, reaching out.

"A little more to the left, girlie," Mrs. Scholz called up over the music she had playing softly in the background.

Christmas music, of course. The only kind almost everyone in Mistletoe knew how to play.

They had bluegrass Christmas music, country Christmas music, gospel Christmas music, Irish folk Christmas music, classical Christmas music, rap and rock Christmas music, and it was everywhere.

Burgundy hadn't realized how much Christmas music there was until she came to Mistletoe.

Or maybe she should say she didn't know how many different times a Christmas song could be remade and in how many different genres of music. And how different it could sound each time it was redone.

The words pretty much stayed the same though, and she could sing them in her head to pretty much every Christmas song ever penned.

There were a lot of them.

Maybe, after she heard it for another year or two, she'd decide on a favorite.

Mrs. Scholz's absolute favorite, though, was "Rockin' Around the Christmas Tree."

Every time it came on, she stopped to dance a little.

Old lady dance, not like breaking some moves on the carpet or anything.

It was cute, and Burgundy enjoyed watching her.

Not that Burgundy ever joined in. The dance moves she knew were way too suggestive. She'd blown by dirty dancing years ago, although "Rockin' Around the Christmas Tree" wasn't exactly music that she'd ever done a striptease to.

But if it paid, she would have done it, much to her shame.

That guilt that she'd been talking to Santa about hit her in the chest again.

She'd been trying to do what he had said, to think about how much God loved her, and how big He was, and how if He'd forgiven her, she should forgive herself.

But she also knew that she needed to feel the guilt. She needed it. If she felt it, Santa was right, it was like pain. It would keep her from going back.

More than anything else in her life, she did not want to go back to what she had been.

So that meant no dancing. She wasn't going to dance and take any kind of chance.

"Get the one on the far left and the one two spaces beside it."

Burgundy put her hand on the knickknacks. The shelf was the highest in the room, and they must have used a forklift to get it up to begin with. Or else this ladder, although whoever that was probably wasn't lucky enough to have Crew at the bottom holding onto it.

Even though he held it tight, it still wobbled, but not enough to make her nervous.

The knickknacks were hideous, in Burgundy's opinion. They looked like stuffed animal dinosaurs crossed with pigs and plastic foam.

Normally, she did whatever Mrs. Scholz said, although every

once in a while, she couldn't help but give her opinion. Design had been an interest of hers before she'd started to sell herself for money.

Clearing her throat, she said, "How about we just take this whole shelf down? I think a little bit of empty space up here will give the room a bigger feel."

She closed her eyes and braced her hands on the wall, waiting to hear Mrs. Scholz's verdict.

"You know, every time you suggest something to me, which you haven't done very often, I like the result. Maybe you should be the one redecorating, and I should be the one listening."

Maybe it was the shock of the words, maybe it was the hint of a compliment that she wasn't used to, or maybe she was just getting old and her body was weak from all the drugs she'd taken when she was younger, but a wave of dizziness hit her, and she bent down, grabbing for the ladder, her arm windmilling, smacking the shelf, and knocking it off the wall along with the knickknacks that were on it.

Most of them fell straight down. One hit Crew in the head. Burgundy cringed. Thankfully, the man had a hard head.

The knickknack wasn't hard; it was a soft plastic. It most likely didn't hurt him.

But she'd managed to hit one of the knickknacks just right to cause it to fly across the room and knock into the music.

Not the music exactly but it hit the volume button somehow so that "Silent Night" started playing at an almost deafening level.

It was just ending though, so it faded away quickly. Mrs. Scholz moved to turn it down as the announcer's voice came on.

"I'm so sorry. I just had a little weird spell there for a minute. I didn't mean to knock everything down."

She looked down. Crew still had his hands on the ladder, and he was braced against it, but there was a small red mark on the side of his forehead where the dinosaur that had been morphing into a pig had hit him.

He glanced up. "Are you okay?"

She didn't expect him to say anything. She didn't expect today to be any different than any other day.

"Maybe you want to get off the ladder for a bit?"

The dizzy spell hit her again, only harder.

The man talked. He talked to her. And he said something nice. She grabbed a hold of the ladder and nodded. "I think I will."

"It's my song!" Mrs. Scholz exclaimed as "Rockin' Around the Christmas Tree" came over the radio.

She started to do the old lady shuffle that had Burgundy grinning every time, shuffling under the ladder and past Crew who still had both hands braced as Burgundy climbed down.

"If you can talk to her, you can dance with me. Come on, you young buck, show this lady your moves." Mrs. Scholz grabbed a hold of Crew's forearm and tugged.

Burgundy was far enough down the ladder that she easily saw Crew's startled expression. Startled, then panicked, and his wide eyes flew all around the room, finally snapping on hers as she looked at him.

She couldn't keep from smiling. He probably didn't appreciate it.

She shrugged. "Mrs. Scholz becomes a wild woman when this song comes on. Mistletoe should ban it." She grinned wider.

"I have to hold the ladder."

"I'm off of it." Burgundy jumped the rest of the way down. "And you're on the hook."

Burgundy went over to the coffee table and sat down on it. The man had talked. Not one sentence but two, and now she was going to watch him dance.

So what if he didn't like it? He deserved the uncomfortableness.

The words of Santa came back to her, suggesting he might be shy. Maybe he was. He was kind of acting like it. Panicked because Mrs. Scholz had asked him to dance. Barking out words, but not unkind words. They were words of caring.

Whoever Santa was, he was a wise man.

She needed to ask Miss Penny the name of the man and get

introduced to him when he didn't have a Santa suit on. She hadn't had too many father figures in her life. She kind of thought that Santa would be a good one.

Plus, being with him felt right. Easy. Comfortable. Like she could spend all evening with him, and he could say things that pushed her and made her think and made her feel guilty, and yet it wasn't a bad thing, but he made her grow. In a good way.

She liked being around him, liked the way he opened her eyes to see that maybe the world wasn't exactly the way she thought it was.

She liked that different perspective.

Crew had let go of the ladder, but he was hesitating as Mrs. Scholz shuffled around him, her hands clasped tight except for pointer fingers which stuck up and poked the air like she was gouging somebody's eyes out as she jerked them around.

Her orthopedic shoes clumped a bit on the hardwood floor as she wiggled, not just her butt, but her waist which seemed to be one line, in an awkward side-to-side diagonal-type direction.

Burgundy had seen some really interesting dancing, had participated in some herself, but Mrs. Scholz was very unique.

"Come on, boy, let's see you bust some moves. Isn't that what the kids say?"

Burgundy snorted, very obvious and in a way that she tried not to do in polite company. In a way she normally didn't do in front of company at all.

She looked around for a tissue. Bust some moves? Mrs. Scholz was hilarious. And here Burgundy had thought she was a stick-in-the-mud when she'd first met her.

Getting up, she walked to the kitchen to get a tissue. Maybe she should just carry the box in, because this was bound to get even more interesting if Mrs. Scholz actually managed to get Crew to dance. If Burgundy didn't wind up rolling on the floor, it would probably be considered a small miracle.

Sure enough, when she came back out of the kitchen, carrying a box of tissues, Crew was doing some kind of shuffle, matching

Mrs. Scholz. Only he didn't have the finger-pointing thing going on.

"Come on, boy, you can do better than that."

Crew put her in mind of a man who was longing with every fiber of his being for a good stiff drink, which made Burgundy wonder about his past and how he'd ended up here.

She'd kind of just assumed he'd grown up in Mistletoe, but she'd never asked anyone.

If he just bought the ranch, then maybe this hadn't been his hometown.

The idea was intriguing.

Mrs. Scholz tapped Crew on his arm. "Loosen up. Nobody here is an expert, and you can't look any worse than I do."

Something flashed across Crew's face, almost as though Mrs. Scholz's words had triggered a memory or maybe a thought. But she could almost see him making himself relax, loosening up.

The change was visual as his limbs loosened, and he started to move to the music.

Wherever the pain was, whatever caused him to limp and gimp like an old man, was still there, but his limbs were more fluid, and she guessed that he'd done a lot of dancing back when he was younger.

By the end of the song, she was convinced he had. The man could dance. And well.

The song ended on a bang. By that time, Mrs. Scholz and Crew were dancing hand in hand. Mrs. Scholz leaned gently back, just shy of vertical, and put one of her orthopedic shoes in the air with a crooked leg. Not exactly *Dancing with the Stars* worthy, but cute nonetheless.

Crew had an arm around her and had his own crazy pose with one knee bent behind her and one leg stretched out straight with his heel on the floor and his big boot sticking up in the air. The hand that wasn't behind her stretched out in the air.

Burgundy wished she had a picture. It would definitely be good for blackmail. At least for Crew.

Mrs. Scholz would probably frame it and hang it beside all the other knickknacks.

Burgundy clapped and laughed. "You guys are amazing. I think you ought to audition for a dancing competition."

"I think we can give those celebrities a run for their money, how about it, kid?" Mrs. Scholz was able to get her foot down, but it took her a little longer to get her back straightened up.

"I think you got me to dance in my living room. Be happy," Crew said, but there was a little smile on his face.

Interesting that his words were directed at Mrs. Scholz but his eyes moved across the room until they met Burgundy's.

She wasn't sure exactly what message he was sending, if any; maybe he just wanted her reaction. She couldn't stop smiling, and she loved the innocence and sweetness and the happiness that had settled down in the living room.

It made her wish that this was her life, her actual life.

And it stirred something else in her. A longing, almost, that had everything to do with the man who just danced with her elderly charge.

Chapter Ten

Crew hefted the bag of donations out of his pickup and gimped over to the collection box beside the secondhand store in Mistletoe.

There were way more knickknacks in his bag than the total population of Mistletoe could possibly ever use, but he supposed it wasn't his problem as to what in the world the people who worked at the secondhand store were going to do with them.

Maybe they had other stores they could farm them out at.

Or maybe with all of the tourists that were coming into Mistletoe lately, there would be enough people who liked...ugly things...to buy them all.

Maybe the store would add a separate wing just for Mrs. Scholz's junk.

He couldn't stop a little friendly grin from brightening his face. The lady had turned out to be sweet. Gruff around the edges, but a sweetness inside. Or maybe her heart just needed love. Kinda like his.

Loosening up a little had been hard but worth it.

Because both of the ladies in the room had smiled when he danced.

He'd tried to remember how he danced when he was drunk. Probably with less coordination, but less concern for how he looked, too. He'd never danced with a girl who'd cared. Usually they were as drunk as he was.

Not anymore. Both of the sober ladies in his living room had seemed to think his performance was okay.

Somehow, that mattered more to him than all the drunk girls in the world.

He lifted the bag up and stuck it in the chute when another vehicle pulled up behind him.

The day was kinda gray and overcast, typical for January in Arkansas, apparently, not that he'd ever spent January in Arkansas before, but the locals said it was typically a cold, gray month, with rain and occasional ice not unexpected.

He didn't mind the cool weather.

Growing up in Texas, Arkansas felt cold, but he was probably more upset at the idea that Valentine's Day was approaching and he really didn't have anybody to spend it with. Really, he knew who he'd like to spend it with, but she didn't seem inclined to want to. She thought he was mean.

He wondered if his dance had done anything to change that. Maybe.

"Crew, good to see you, man. How's it going?"

Crew finished pushing the bag in and turned to see his former coworker and one of his best friends pulling his own much smaller bag out of his pickup. "Going good. This must be honey-do list day?" That was making the assumption he had a honey, which he didn't. Mrs. Scholz definitely did not count as a honey. Dance partner in his living room...okay. Honey? Not likely.

As crippled as he was, he was more likely to be partnered up with Mrs. Scholz than with the one he wanted.

Did he want her? Really want her? That was kind of a new thought. He'd have to think about that.

"I've got one a mile long. You?"

"This is it. Well, and some paint at the hardware store."

"I already made the hardware store run, and I had to get a lot more than paint." Denver grinned, jerking his head at his pickup. "When I get to the grocery store, I'll need an overweight permit for that thing."

"You're the one with five kids. You should have thought of this, man. It's called planning."

"Well..." Denver looked at the ground, a little smile tilting the corners of his mouth. "It's five...for now."

"You're kidding?" Crew felt like his grin was jumping off his face. "Natalie is expecting?"

Denver nodded. His grin exploded into a smile, a proud smile that showed just how excited and happy he was.

"You're crazy, man. Six kids?" But then he thought of Burgundy, and Mrs. Scholz, and the way his house had felt when they had been laughing together. He thought again of Levi and the happy chaos in his home. Maybe six kids wasn't such a bad idea. "Never mind. I can see the appeal."

Denver's smile changed just a bit. "You found someone, didn't you?" He smacked his shoulder with one hand while he threw his bag into the collection box with the other. "Who is she? Do I know her?"

Crew shook his head. "You know me. How in the world would I say enough words to a woman to get her to look at me twice?"

He didn't need to tell Denver that he'd been working on it. He definitely didn't need to tell Denver that if he dressed up in a Santa Claus outfit, he was finally able to talk to a girl, only she thought he was an old man.

"You know the right woman can bring the best of a man out. It's kind of funny how that works. I guess, when you experience it, you'll know what I mean," Denver said in a softer tone and one that Crew hadn't heard him use too often.

It was laced with affection and maybe a little adoration. He'd say his friend was smitten, and that was true. Obviously he was.

But he didn't mean that in an unkind way.

"I suppose you know what you're talking about," he said finally.

There was no doubting the sincerity of his friend's look and the anticipation of his smile when he talked about his wife expecting.

Crew hardly thought that that would ever be him, but Denver wouldn't fake it. He just wasn't that kind of man.

"I'd better get going. Got a lot of things left on my honey-do list." He patted his pocket. "Somehow I even get my mom putting things on my honey-do list." He shook his head. "How do some people grow out of that, and I never have?"

"Maybe that's because you haven't been home for the last fifteen years. Your mom's probably just making up for lost time." It was a little bit of a joke, but they really hadn't been home much. Life on the ship was all-encompassing, and a man couldn't just take a day off and drive home.

Maybe it was guilt, he didn't know, but he said, "Is there anything I can help you with?"

Denver gave him a squinted look. "I've heard you've been doing enough. Or at least you've gotten roped into it. And no, my mom has decided that starting a pen pal thing with people who are in the hospital for months on end is a really good idea. Because of the name Mistletoe, she thought it would be fun for people in hospitals to send letters to us. So she's looking for volunteers to write letters to people. Unless you're interested in that?" He raised a brow.

Crew shook his head. No way. "I'll talk to Mrs. Scholz. She might be interested in writing letters."

One side of Denver's mouth tilted up. "That's what I thought. Any luck on the farm?"

Denver had helped him secure the financing for the farm, and Crew had confided in him that he wasn't sure he was going to be able to do the work necessary to make the money needed to make the payments. But at that point in his life, he figured it didn't matter if he took the chance. The financing had gone through, based on the previous years' profit/loss sheets.

"I found out I'm definitely not going to be able to do what I need to. I haven't got around to hiring anyone."

"I'll keep an ear out for a good worker. I'll let you know if I hear anything."

"Appreciate that. Your dad's on top of things too. He found someone for Mrs. Scholz." Crew kept his face carefully blank. He might have a little crush or something weird going on about Burgundy. But she definitely didn't have anything on him. He didn't want to embarrass himself.

"I heard about that." Denver looked thoughtful. "Mrs. Scholz will be good for her. It sounded to me like she needed a safe place to land."

They shook hands and parted ways, with Crew wondering what in the world Denver could have meant by that last comment.

Chapter Eleven

Burgundy sat beside Santa in the buggy. She'd been looking forward to tonight for a while, ever since Miss Penny had called and asked if she would be interested.

She and Santa—she still didn't know who he was despite having asked around at church and hinted to Miss Penny, but Miss Penny had smiled and shaken her head—had gone on several other short trips, directly in the town of Mistletoe.

Which was the reason she was looking forward to tonight. It was another long trip. The ones in the town of Mistletoe hadn't exactly been conducive to the kind of conversation they'd had the first night they'd spent together. She thought about things that they talked about and the way she felt, and the way he'd made her think, and wanted that again.

Definitely the feeling. That feeling of rightness when she'd been with him.

She didn't want to term it a romantic feeling. After all, Santa was forty years older than she was, and she had never been into older men. No more than she had to be, although in her working days, she'd done whatever the director dictated. Anything to earn a paycheck.

But those days were behind her.

She refused to think about this as a romance, but more as a... friendship that satisfied her soul.

She kinda hoped Santa felt the same. He seemed happy to see her, although it was always hard to tell with the way his beard covered his face, then those glasses that hid all but the color of his eyes.

They were the same color as Crew's.

She might have wondered if they were related, but Crew never had any visitors, and she never saw Santa around town, so she kinda thought not.

"Do you go to the church in Mistletoe? Pastor Race's church?"

She did assume that he did. How else would he have gotten this job?

Santa held the reins loosely in his hand. He didn't seem quite as hunched over tonight. It was slightly warmer, and maybe that made the difference.

Finally, he said, "I do."

"I looked for you in church, and I didn't see you."

"I'm there. Sometimes we don't see what's actually in front of us because it's not what we're looking for."

"What's that supposed to mean? You're actually a woman?" She said it to be a little bit smart because she didn't like the way he'd answered her question with a riddle.

He gave her a side glance as the horses plodded out of town, leaving the last of the streetlights behind them. Not that there were that many streetlights.

"Would that bother you?"

Of course. She hadn't been terming their relationship romance exactly, but she didn't want to feel like this toward a woman.

That gave her pause.

Why? Why did he give her pause? She'd just told herself it wasn't a romance.

Her shoulders slumped; she couldn't stop them. She didn't want it to be a romance. But for some reason, it was important to her that Santa was a man.

"Well, of course. Whoever heard of a female Santa? Of course, I would be disappointed if you were a woman."

"Well, I won't disappoint you...that way anyway."

Her head jerked around. The insinuation was he would disappoint her in other ways.

"Well, you're not the only one that's disappointed a lot of people. There are a lot of things about me that if you knew you'd be more than disappointed. Disgusted might be a better word."

She hadn't meant to say that much. She wanted to be friends. She wanted that right feeling. She wanted that feeling like he was the perfect person for her to be with at this point in her life. She didn't want to open any of those doors in her mind that were closed and locked and padlocked and double padlocked. Doors she never wanted to open again.

But she just walked up to them.

"Maybe we both have skeletons in our closet. Isn't that what that is?"

"No. A skeleton in my closet would be a welcome thing. Compared to what I've done."

Why did she keep insinuating about how bad she was? Why couldn't she just keep her mouth shut?

There was something about him that made her want to be honest.

Lying had been easy in her old life. It still was easier now. She still, quite often, had to fight against the temptation to lie.

But now? She was trying not to tell the truth and couldn't do anything but.

It had to be the man.

"I don't think I want to compare pasts with you. Because I think you'd be surprised. Let's talk about something else."

She hardly thought his past was worse than hers, but she said, "I think that's a great idea."

If they didn't want to talk about their pasts, what better thing to talk about than the future, right?

"So, what are your plans for the rest of your life? You'd be Santa Claus forever?" She hoped that wasn't a depressing question for him. She supposed, as he got further and further along in his life, it felt less about the future, more about the past.

Or maybe just about the present.

She wasn't sure.

She hadn't gotten to that point in her life yet. Although, some of the things that she'd done when she was younger had made her age faster. Sometimes she felt like an old lady.

"This isn't too bad. I kind of like it. It's a little addicting to show up at someone's door, see their shock and surprise, then eventually their happiness. I'd say it should pay a little better, because it'd be nice to do full-time, but it's the kind of thing that you just want to do for free because it's so much fun."

His voice, always gruff and kind of old mannish, had a familiar ring to it that she couldn't quite place.

For some reason, Crew came to mind. He was talking a little more. Saying "good morning" and "how are you."

And, starting to think about Crew, he gave her the same feeling that this man did. Maybe that's why she would have been so upset if Santa had been a woman. Just that feeling of rightness. Like sitting down at the supper table and seeing him across from her was exactly how life should be.

Of course, it couldn't really be like that. He was managing to talk to her, and he was definitely managing to talk to Mrs. Scholz. They almost had full conversations over the supper table. But he still seemed to be forcing himself to talk.

That's probably the way it would always be. It was almost like he knew what she was, but he was putting up with her anyway. Because she did take good care of Mrs. Scholz. She'd also uncluttered his house almost completely. They were ready to paint.

"What about you?" Santa's voice startled her. She hadn't realized she'd gone silent.

"I'm sorry. I just kind of stopped talking there, didn't I?" She leaned back and adjusted herself in the seat. They were cushioned and comfortable. "I think it's because I'm so comfortable with you. I just don't feel like I have to keep talking or that I have to be anything other than what I am. It's weird. I'm sorry."

He grunted, but she was pretty sure it pleased him.

"And I agree with you. This is so much fun. The houses that we've been in, the way the people look at us, when their eyes light up, and the expressions of wonder and joy on their faces, and they say, 'but it's not even Christmas!' And then they say this is what you get for living in a town called Mistletoe." Her breath huffed out. "It's just so much fun to see that happiness and know we're a part of it. So I agree. I'd love to get paid for doing it, but it's the kind of thing that I don't need to get paid for in order to want to do it."

"I kind of figured you felt the same way. I watched your face some. It's…beautiful to see."

He said that last bit like he was a little embarrassed to say it, and maybe he was worried that she thought it might be a bit inappropriate for a man of his age to say to her.

"Thank you." He wasn't calling her classically beautiful; he was calling her beautiful on the inside. And that meant more. Especially considering what she used to be on her inside.

"So what are *your* plans for the future?"

"I did notice that you sidestepped my question."

"What old man has plans for the future? I plan to live until I die."

"Would you be satisfied with an answer like that from me?"

"You have your whole life in front of you. Surely you want to do something besides live in Mistletoe and take care of an old lady for the rest of it?"

"I feel like I've lived enough life already. I'm pretty happy with Mrs. Scholz and Crew."

"Last time I talked about Crew, you weren't very happy with him."

"You know, I thought about what you said. I thought you might be right. Maybe he really is shy. But, with that said, he's kind of relaxed around us a little more. I still don't think he likes me very much, but he's been getting along really well with Mrs. Scholz. It's fun to watch them banter with each other across the table. She's kind of a crusty old lady, with a soft inside, and he's almost the same. They joke back and forth. They really seem to hit it off."

"Why are they even living together?"

"Apparently that farm was Mrs. Scholz's husband's. She wasn't able to keep it, couldn't afford to. She had to sell. But one of the stipulations of her signing the title over was that she got to stay until she died." Burgundy's voice softened. "Apparently, Crew is concerned about her mental capacity, her ability to take care of things, and he wanted her to have a caretaker."

"So he was taking care of her?"

It was almost like Santa was pointing that out to her so that she would see that Crew wasn't all bad.

"You know you don't have to try to sell me on him. I'm actually kinda starting to like him myself." She found it was true.

There was a stunned silence, then Santa said, "Oh?"

"You don't have to sound so shocked." She tapped his shoulder with her fist. "He's actually kind of a nice guy. When you think about the things he's done. You should have seen him dancing with Mrs. Scholz. They were hilarious. I kind of..."

"Yeah?"

"Nothing."

"It was something."

"It was looking stupid. I guess I just don't really know how to dance with innocence. You know?" She was giving away way too much of her past, and she plowed on without stopping to give him a chance to ask about that. "I mean, I guess I saw them dancing, and I thought, I wouldn't mind dancing with him. Dancing like that. In a fun, sweet way, with no worries about how you look, and no worries about being sexy or whatever it is that people try to be when they dance. It...took me back to a time that I guess I never even lived through. Because even in my childhood, dancing was different."

Santa didn't say anything, and she wished she'd not said so much. The horses clopped on while she wished she could get out and run awhile. It would be hard to do in her elf uniform, but she thought seriously about it.

She'd embarrassed herself.

"And watching him dance made you like him?"

She laughed. Leave it to Santa to make her feel better. "No. That's not it. I guess I just saw him in a new light after you said he might be shy. I thought less of him not liking me and more about him being intimidated by me. That changes things, you know? It made him feel more approachable. And maybe he became more approachable because that's how I treated him? But he's not too bad to look at either."

"Really? I'll have to check him out. You know, in an old man kind of way."

She giggled again. Funny how Santa could get her to giggle. Man, if her old friends could see her now, giggling over such a stupid thing. They would definitely laugh at her. Except, most of them were not still around, since they were pretty much all addicted to drugs, some homeless, a couple of them in jail. She didn't know anyone who was happy and successful with a "normal" life.

Not even her.

"Back in high school, I suppose girls would have called him dreamy."

"I thought he was all stoved up?" He asked the question cautiously, like he didn't want to offend her by insinuating that Crew might not be everything she was saying he was.

"I guess I forget about that. I mean I know I see it, but I guess it's not something that matters to me. Or maybe I see that there's more to him than that. Like, there's a man with feelings under that gruff exterior, and I associate his gimpiness with his exterior. It doesn't have anything to do with what's inside."

"Really? Interesting. I don't want to offend you, but most of the girls I've talked to seem to be a little more shallow than that. Like a man has to have the right amount of muscles and the right shoulder width, and for goodness' sake, he has to be tall. With lots of hair." Santa reached his hand up and rubbed over his hat. "At least I have that last one down. Even though it's the wrong color."

She laughed. "I don't give a flip about his hair. Or shoulders. Or how skinny or not skinny he is. Although, like I said, Crew is dreamy. But I suppose there's different ways for a man to be dreamy. It doesn't really have anything to do with the way he looks. Dancing with Mrs. Scholz? That was dreamy."

"I guess I'll have to find an old lady to dance with."

She laughed again. "Santa, you're funny. You're dreamy. When you hold all those kids in your lap. That was dreamy. I'll have to introduce you to Mrs. Scholz. She'll think you're dreamy."

"Too much age difference?"

"Yeah. A romantic relationship ruins friendship anyway." At least it had every single time in her life. They'd ruined business relationships too. She'd had some of those that had turned romantic, and they had been a big fail.

Of course, her business wasn't exactly the same as everyone else's. Maybe normal people could do that. It might be fun to sleep with the boss and be married to him too. In fact, she thought maybe working with her husband would be almost as good as being friends with him.

Another time, another life. She'd kind of ruined this one.

"I guess I disagree with that."

"What?"

"I think the best kind of romantic relationships are where you have a good solid friendship underneath, holding everything together. I think you have to like each other before you can love each other."

That was noble. But then, that's what she expected from Santa, wasn't it? That's what he'd done the last time, turned her beliefs on their head. It gave her new things to think about. Questioning the accepted wisdom of the day.

"I need to think about that. You might be right."

"I guess this is where I promise not to tell Crew you said he was dreamy."

"You better not. I'll never talk to you again."

"Really?"

"That's probably not true, but it sounds good."

"It sounds awful."

The lights for the house where Mr. and Mrs. Foote lived appeared in the distance. There was a little cluster of houses, and theirs was on the end.

"That's our stop. It looks like they're still up. I wasn't sure, because of Mrs. Foote's surgery. They might go to bed early."

"I'm sorry. We're late because of me. I don't like to leave Mrs. Scholz until she's gone to bed for the night. Or at least upstairs to her room, and that's usually around seven."

"It's okay. The food isn't for tonight anyway."

They didn't say any more until he pulled up to the house. Santa clambered down and painfully tied the horses to the banister while Burgundy gathered up the disposable aluminum casserole pans they'd brought the meal in.

They walked up the steps together.

Chapter Twelve

Crew knocked on the door while Burgundy stood beside him. This had become something he enjoyed. Not just enjoyed, but looked forward to. He hadn't been joking when he said he'd do it for free. But he didn't want to do it by himself. And he didn't want to do it with just anyone.

He wanted to do it with Burgundy.

He couldn't imagine doing it with anyone else.

Of course it would work out. Things always did.

Still, he could have preferences. His preference was Burgundy.

He raised his hand and knocked again, exchanging a look with Burgundy.

Usually people came to the door and were shocked to see Santa. But no one was coming. He rapped again, then said, "She had surgery, hip replacement maybe? I don't remember."

"Yes. That's what they said. Hip replacement. But Mr. Foote should be there."

"Maybe he's taking a shower or something."

A voice hollered weakly through the door, "Door's open. Come on in."

They exchanged another glance, with raised brows and uneasy smiles. This was different. For sure.

Somehow, having Burgundy beside him made different okay.

He opened the door and smirked at her. "Ladies first."

She smirked right back. "That's kind of overrated. How about I get the door for you?" She was just goofing off, though, because she walked by him and into the house.

He couldn't wipe the silly grin off his face. Thankfully, the Santa Claus beard that he had was very full and very curly, and she'd never even suspected, as far as he knew, that he was Crew.

His face fell, though, as they walked in. Mrs. Foote sat on a recliner, her face sallow and pinched.

Burgundy had gone straight toward her, setting the casserole she carried on the coffee table as she passed it.

Crew shut the door behind him and gimped over, frowning in concern.

Mrs. Foote did not look good.

Still, her smile was sincere. "It's so nice of you guys to come. Santa Claus and it's not even Christmas. That's nice." Mrs. Foote's voice was weak and thready, but her kindly eyes crinkled with genuine gratefulness.

"Ho ho ho, Merry Christmas," Crew said, as he always did when they walked in. But his voice just wasn't as jolly as it had been previous times. She obviously was not doing well, and he wasn't sure what to do about it.

Thankfully, Burgundy was already beside her, kneeling.

"Is there something I can do for you, Mrs. Foote?" Burgundy asked, setting her hand on top of Mrs. Foote's hand and squeezing.

"Clarence is around, and he's...helping...me."

At her hesitation, Burgundy's eyes slipped to his, questions in them.

He wasn't sure whether his eyes held questions or anger.

Obviously, Mr. Foote—Clarence—wasn't doing a very good job of looking after his wife, who seemed like a really sweet lady.

Of course, appearances could be deceiving.

He took up the casserole dishes, and balancing them in one hand so he could use his cane with the other, he carried them out to the kitchen, listening as Burgundy gently asked Mrs. Foote some questions about her medications and her pain levels.

Mrs. Foote had replied that she'd like a glass of sweet tea, so Crew called out that he'd get it. After setting the casseroles on the counter, he dug in the cupboards for a glass, grabbed the pitcher from the refrigerator, and filled it up.

It was nice to play Santa, because he got to use a cane, which definitely eased some of the pain in his hips. But it wasn't anything that he would ever use without the Santa uniform on.

He'd claim far and wide that it was a prop. No one would ever drag out of him that he actually preferred walking with it.

As he walked back in, he noticed the closed doors at the end of the living room which he hadn't seen before. There seemed to be some noise coming from behind them, and he glanced over as he walked by.

Blue light flickered, like there was a TV or computer being used. He didn't look long and kept walking, not wanting to be rude, to stare, or to be nosy.

"Here's your tea, Mrs. Foote," he said, leaning down with the glass.

"Oh, thank you so much, Santa. I think I'm supposed to have milk and cookies for you? I'm sorry."

"That's only Christmas. When I show up unannounced any other time of the year, you're off the hook." That had been his standard line any time someone had felt bad for not having the typical milk and cookies that they felt Santa expected.

Mrs. Foote wiggled in her chair. "I need to sit up a little."

She leaned forward. Burgundy reached over to adjust her blanket. Crew wasn't sure exactly what happened, but somehow Mrs. Foote jerked, her hand trembled, and the glass fell and spilled all over Burgundy's elf top.

Burgundy squealed and jumped up. Grabbing the back of her shirt, she pulled it up. She had a shirt on underneath it, which she was probably trying to keep from getting wet, but it came up with the elf costume.

Not a whole lot, but enough for Crew to see the tattoo on her back.

It was an elephant, lifelike and huge, taking up her entire lower back, its legs disappearing into the waistband of her pants.

An unusual tattoo that he'd only seen one time before.

Not in real life. It had been on the screen. Before he'd been saved.

During that part of his life that he wished he could forget. But the images were burned in his brain. Including that one.

The movie hadn't been one that a man could take his family to see. It wasn't one that he'd ever watch with his friends.

It was the kind of movie a man watched by himself, late at night when no one else would know or see what wickedness he was doing.

Burgundy straightened, pulling her elf shirt the rest of the way over her head with one hand and tugging down on her undershirt with the other.

Things clicked into place.

Why she'd seemed so familiar to him. Why she was so ashamed of her past. Why she hadn't wanted to talk about it. Why she thought there was no future.

His breath was shallow, and he hadn't figured out what to think. His shock was so deep he couldn't move if the house had been on fire. He couldn't move when her eyes landed on his, a little grin touching her face, still laughing about the tea, not realizing what he'd seen. And that he'd recognized it.

It didn't take long. He couldn't get his face to show anything else.

Maybe there was hurt there. He certainly felt it.

Not just for her, for himself.

The fact that he knew exactly where he'd seen that before, and she would have to know. He couldn't believe, wouldn't have guessed, had no idea, didn't know what to say, didn't know what to do, didn't know how to act.

Realization dawned in her eyes as she watched his face.

She couldn't see it. It was covered by the beard, but she had to read everything she needed to know in his eyes.

At least she didn't know it was him.

She thought it was Santa who had seen her in that movie.

She probably didn't even know which movie.

He remembered clearly that she'd been billed as a star, "performing" in many movies. Using the word "movie" loosely. There wasn't too much to them. Definitely they didn't waste money on a wardrobe person.

Shock froze her face. It slipped into betrayal. She'd thought Santa was better than that.

She couldn't hold him accountable when she was just as guilty as he, could she?

Her lips tightened before she turned away from him, pointedly pulling her shirt down and tossing her elf shirt on the coffee table.

"I'm sorry, Mrs. Foote. We seem to have bumped into each other. Are you okay?"

"It's my fault. I'm just a little weak yet, and I shouldn't have been holding the tea while I was trying to move."

Crew shook himself and forced his lips to work. "It was my fault. I should have held the tea until you were ready for it." He remembered just in the nick of time to keep his voice pitched low like he'd been doing for Santa, making it sound like an old man's voice as much as he could.

"I guess we're all taking the blame for it," Mrs. Foote said diplomatically. "I'm kind of wet. It would be nice to change. Would you mind?" She looked at Burgundy.

Crew grabbed the glass off the coffee table. "I'll take this back out to the kitchen and fill it up. You can let me know when you're ready."

"We'll do that," Burgundy said, a decided frost in her voice that had never been there before.

Man, he was such an idiot.

He wasn't sure exactly what made him an idiot though. Falling for an ex-porn star, or being shocked that she was one, or acting like there was something wrong with her when he was just as guilty.

This wasn't the time to talk about it, though.

He could hardly wait to get her back out to the buggy. He needed to explain to her that it wasn't her.

But...he'd never considered. Never thought.

Did it make a difference?

He filled the glass up without even thinking about it and set it on the counter before leaning against the countertop himself.

From what he'd seen of her, since she'd been living in his house, she wasn't doing that anymore. She hadn't talked about any current counseling, hadn't talked about anything other than a few mentions of saving her salary and eventually buying a little cottage of her own. He seemed to recall Mrs. Scholz and her talking about that.

Man, if he'd thought she wouldn't take him before, she definitely wouldn't take him now.

He supposed with enough alcohol, he'd been smooth, or at least with enough alcohol in him and his partner, he'd been smooth. He didn't know. But a porn star?

Could he fall for a porn star?

He felt like he already had.

Maybe the question should be could she fall for someone who used to watch the movies that she made? And had been part of the reason that she'd become what she had?

That was probably the question.

"Santa?" Burgundy's voice held concern and a slight edge of panic.

He jerked his head up immediately. "What?"

"I think we need to call an ambulance. She's burning up with fever, and it looks like her incision is infected."

The next hour went by in a blur. Mistletoe wasn't exactly a big city, and all ambulance crews were volunteer.

Once the crew got there, they took over, and he stood back with Burgundy, but neither of them said anything. Through all the noise and moving her around, finally getting her on a stretcher, Mr. Foote never did show up.

Finally, as they were wheeling her out the door, he stood at her side and said, "Do you think your husband needs to be notified?"

"Wait until I'm gone. He's in that room off to the side. He'll probably be upset to be interrupted."

That was weird.

Crew looked at Burgundy, but she wouldn't meet his gaze. Keeping her eyes cast down, like the ground was really interesting. Maybe she was looking at the doorjamb.

He wanted to take a hold of her and shake her. To let her know that that's exactly how he felt too. After all, if he hadn't watched her movie, he wouldn't have recognized her tattoo.

Surely she knew that. But it looked like she was blaming herself for everything.

He waited until the ambulance motor started and the lights turned on before he turned.

"I'm going to say something to Mr. Foote. Then you're ready to go?"

Her chin came up, and her head nodded, but her eyes still went to the side. She wouldn't meet his gaze.

He strode across the living room, in his head anyway. In reality, his cane thumped as he limped across the living room, his hips hurting more than they usually did. Burgundy went by him, into the kitchen, and grabbed the casseroles.

He assumed she was putting them in the refrigerator.

He tapped on the door that he'd noticed earlier. He could see the blue light flashing through the crack. There was no answer to his tap.

He rapped harder. Still no answer.

He opened the door slowly, intending to put his head in and at least tell the man his wife had gone to the emergency room.

Interesting that she hadn't wanted him to know until she was gone.

It didn't take long after he opened the door to figure out why.

It wasn't Burgundy on the screen, but it was the same kind of movie that Crew used to watch. Mr. Foote stared at the screen, his face flushed, a bottle of beer on the tray in front of him and at least four or five empty bottles lying around.

That answered all Crew's questions.

"Your wife just went to the ER."

Mr. Foote blinked but didn't take his eyes off the TV set.

Crew was grateful for the dimness of the room. He didn't want to see any more than what he already had. He backed out, closing the door, standing there with his head down, his hand on the knob.

That's what he used to be. But for the grace of God, it could be him again.

He, and men like him and Mr. Foote, were the reason Burgundy cried at night.

He smelled the peppermint before he turned. She stood right there.

He saw on her face that she knew exactly what was going on in that room.

"Let's go." He put his hand on her shoulder, the first time he'd reached out to touch her, and she jerked away, grabbing her elf shirt from the coffee table and striding out ahead of him.

The horses had a good rest, and normally he would have been looking forward to the long ride home and a sweet conversation with Burgundy.

He'd never talked to anyone so easily in his life before. Never had a conversation that was all over the place, where they could talk about anything. Spiritual stuff, fun stuff, future plans. The only thing they hadn't talked about was their pasts.

Now they were laid out in front of them.

Of course, she didn't know who he really was. But she knew what he'd done.

He'd been having an easier time talking to her at home. But he doubted he'd be able to talk about this without the Santa suit.

He drove the horses out of the driveway and onto the road before he tried to say anything.

He had his mouth open to start but then realized she was hunched over and probably cold.

"Hold these." He didn't make it a question but a command as he handed the reins over. She took them out of instinct.

"But I can't drive!"

"Just a minute." He took his Santa suit jacket off, shaking it before he draped it around her shoulders. She hunched into it without saying anything, pulling the ends together, ducking down, and curling up like she could hide in it.

He took the reins back. She gave them easily but didn't look at him or speak.

"About what happened back there—"

"I don't want to talk about it." She didn't give him a chance to say anything more.

"Maybe I do."

"Maybe you don't have the right."

"I'm sorry. I guess I kinda thought we were friends."

"I guess you kinda thought wrong." She yanked the coat tighter and looked away from him.

He didn't think it was the fact that the Santa suit was gone. She still didn't know who he was, but she knew *what* he was.

Or at least what he had been.

And he couldn't find words to tell her anything different.

Chapter Thirteen

urgundy stepped outside, the tears already coming down her cheeks. She'd given Santa his jacket back, jumped in her car, and driven away. Normally, she offered to drive him home. He always refused, limping around the side of the church. She assumed he lived somewhere in town.

She'd been tempted to try to find out where a couple of times. But she'd respected his privacy.

When he trusted her, he'd tell her.

But he'd recognized her tattoo. He knew who she was.

She'd been embarrassed, more embarrassed than she'd ever been in her life. This was supposed to be a new life; her old life wasn't supposed to follow her.

Be sure your sin will find you out.

She hated that verse. She had so much sin to be found.

It was supposed to be buried. It was supposed be gone.

God forgets, but you reap what you sow.

She hated that verse too. Why couldn't she just start over with a clean slate? She was sorry for what she'd done.

She knew she was forgiven; why couldn't it just go away?

He's just as guilty as you are. He watched it.

She didn't even know why she cared. She didn't even know his name. Why did it matter to her?

Because she thought they were friends. She thought they were good friends. She felt like she had a special bond with him that she didn't have with anyone else, no matter his age.

He reminded her of what Crew might be when he was that age. If he ever learned to talk, which he seemed to have been doing as he got more comfortable with them.

She snuggled Rosemary closer to her as the tears flowed down her cheeks.

She felt so dirty.

Like she could never be clean. All of those pictures of her were still out there. All the movies were still there. People could still watch. People like Mr. Foote could neglect his wife while sitting in front of the TV set and watch people do vile and awful things and somehow get a charge out of it.

Those movies were never going away. There would always be those people who would see that tattoo on her back and know who she was.

She'd looked into tattoo removal when she was in rehab. It was way more expensive than what she could afford.

Definitely working for minimum wage with Mrs. Scholz wasn't going to enable her to get a tattoo of that size removed anytime soon.

She was stuck. But she'd covered it. She'd been so careful.

She had relaxed her guard.

Normally she kept her hand at her mouth, so she wouldn't make any noise, or at least tried to keep it down, but she just couldn't. She felt like her heart was broken, not just shattered into a million tiny pieces, but it cut everywhere it touched. Breathing hurt.

She needed to leave. She couldn't stay in this town. Santa was sure to tell everyone. He didn't need to tell everyone.

All he had to do was tell one person who would tell everyone. He couldn't keep something like that to himself. It was gossip too good to not share.

Wrapping her arms around Rosemary, she clutched her to her chest and doubled over, crying as hard as she'd ever cried before, knowing it wouldn't do any good, wouldn't make her feel any better. The shower she took when she was done wouldn't help either.

She didn't know how long she had been crying before she realized there was a presence behind her.

She thought later, maybe it was the scent that had given her the hint.

It's what she'd come to associate with Santa Claus, hot chocolate and coffee mixed with wintergreen. Crew smelled almost the exact same way.

And that's who she was expecting to see when she turned, only it wasn't.

Santa stood behind her.

She shook her head. "Go away!"

She turned her back on him, sobbing harder. Unable to stop. She'd never been able to stop.

Not until she was too exhausted to cry more.

It took at least an hour, and she wasn't nearly done. She sobbed, hard, uncontrollably, clutching Rosemary to her stomach and bending over. She dropped to her knees, her back to Santa, praying that he'd leave, leave her alone, leave her to sink in the disgusting mess that was her past. Leave her to the guilt that she felt for every movie she'd ever made, for the marriages she'd destroyed, for the lives she'd ruined, for the addictions she'd fostered. For the boys she'd corrupted.

So much evil she'd been involved in, so much. And there was nothing she could do about it.

She sobbed harder. A hand landed on her back. It felt right, warm, and everything she wanted, and she shook it off. She couldn't stand it any more now than she could earlier this evening. He couldn't touch her. She was filthy.

"Don't touch me!" Her words were loud and unnatural and filled with pain and the crying and guilt and shame, and the voice was almost unrecognizable as hers. "Go away!"

"I'm not going anywhere."

She turned to scream at him, through her tears, but when she turned, he was taking his beard off.

"I live here."

He couldn't have shocked her more if he'd punched her in the stomach.

All the bluster went out of her. In front of her shocked eyes, his beard was taken off along with the glasses and the hat, and Crew stood there.

She should have known. How did she not know?

Stupid was the word that defined her life. It was the only word that could define her life. That's what she'd been all of her life. And now was no different.

She ran back through the things she'd told Santa. The things he knew, that Crew knew.

No wonder the feelings were the same. No wonder she felt that same sense of warmth and peace and rightness with him. He was the same person.

She shook her head, couldn't do anything but shake her head, harder and harder, until finally she was sobbing again, and turned her back on him once more, curling over, not able to do anything but cry.

She didn't even have the strength to shake him off when his hand touched her shoulder again.

At least her current sobs were quiet; she wasn't wailing like she'd been doing before.

"Please let me hold you. You've done this every night since you've come, and it's killed me every single time. Please?"

She didn't say yes. But she didn't shake his hand off, and she didn't move away when it went from one shoulder to the other until his arm was around her, and his other hand pushed the side of her head into his chest, and he knelt with her there, holding her head and shoulders while she cried.

CREW'S HIPS ACHED, and his knees and shoulders burned. He kind of felt like it was penance though. Like he deserved it. To feel the pain.

To think that what he used to be had created what he held in front of him now. That kind of man, the kind of man who saw a woman as an object or as some kind of slimy entertainment. Who would pay money to see things done, things that were private and sacred and blessed only in the bonds of marriage. If there weren't men like him, there wouldn't be women like Burgundy.

This pain wouldn't be real, she wouldn't be feeling it now, and he wouldn't be sitting here helpless. Helpless to help her, helpless to know what to do.

He hated that feeling. Hated the feeling of not being able to do something.

All his life, he could work with his hands, fixing things, seeing the problems, and working the solutions out in his head. Knowing the danger, calculating the risk, and figuring out how to implement the solution.

Since his accident, his physical prowess had been reduced, and that had been hard enough.

But it was nothing compared to this. Seeing this woman, broken in front of him, and not knowing how to help her. And knowing part of her brokenness was his fault.

There were more like her. That was a new thought, and it hit him hard.

Burgundy wasn't the only woman that he created. There were hundreds more like her, maybe even thousands. Who knew?

"I'm sorry," he whispered, not knowing what else to say, wishing he could help. But just knowing he needed to apologize. "I'm so sorry."

She wasn't sobbing anymore, and her back didn't shake, but her face was still wet and pressed against him. She still held her elephant tight.

A sad reminder that the woman who looked so capable and strong was just as weak and vulnerable as anyone else. As a child even.

He wanted to fix it, knew he couldn't.

"There's nothing you can do." Her voice was husky and soft and bitter.

"Part of the reason you're like this is because of me."

"You can't take responsibility for the sins of mankind. And what I've done is not your fault." Despite her tears, her words were strong and still laced with bitterness.

"If there weren't men like me, you wouldn't have had a job."

"You're one man. There's tens of thousands of them out there."

"Don't I know it."

"You can't take responsibility for them all."

"No. But I can take responsibility for me. It's because of me, and men like me, yes, that this is broken." He pointed without touching at where her heart beat in her chest.

"I don't have one of those."

"Everyone does. Don't give me that baloney."

"It's not baloney. It's the truth."

"Then why are you crying?" His voice had risen from a whisper to almost a normal tone.

"Because I'm dirty. Because I've led so many people astray. Because it caused contention in marriages. Because I've caused divorce. Because I've contaminated innocent eyes, and because mothers have cried over their sons because of me. Wives cry over their husbands. Grandfathers molest their grandchildren because of what they see me doing. That's why I'm crying."

"You're giving yourself an awful lot of credit, aren't you?"

"Every word is true."

"You are not responsible for all that. There is a whole industry and a whole consumer segment that runs that industry along with supplying the greenbacks it takes to make it successful. It is not you. Stop making yourself bigger than what you are."

Her head came up, and her eyes narrowed at him. He could almost see the wheels turning in her head.

"What I've done is wrong."

"Not arguing that. Was." His eyes roved over her face. "What I've done was wrong, too." His voice softened. "There's nothing we can do about it. Nothing we can do about the past. We've talked about it before, remember?"

She nodded. "Because God is so big, and God is so good, God is so awesome, and because He loved us, we serve Him."

He nodded. "And?"

"That makes it all the more amazing that our sins are forgiven."

"You believe that, don't you?"

"I have no other explanation for how I got out of what I got out of other than God. It's a miracle. Straight out. I have to believe. Because to not believe in God would be to not believe in what happened to me."

He nodded. "I can probably say the same thing." He grunted. "God sent Denver, who helped me out of the life I was living. But when I had the accident that did this to me," his hand gestured up and down his body, "I shouldn't have survived. I don't know how else to explain how I got out of there other than God did it." He looked away. "I guess that'll make a believer of anyone."

She jerked her head like she agreed, then she looked straight ahead before slowly laying her head back down on his chest.

It was such a little thing, her head on his chest, but the idea that she knew what he'd done, and she knew he knew what she'd done... it represented so much trust to him he could hardly contain it in his chest.

His arms tightened around her. "There's something about you

that gives me peace, a warmth, a rightness in my chest when I'm around you. Like an absolute. Like you were made to be here. With me."

"You can't mean that. You just found out tonight what I am."

"I found out what you *were*. Am I wrong?"

"I hope not. I don't have any desire to go back. What you said about the guilt, it really struck true with me. It's the pain that reminds me I don't want to be what I was."

"And that's all I need to hear. I certainly have no right to hold you to any kind of higher standard than me."

He couldn't help but notice, though, she hadn't said the same thing about him. That his past didn't matter to her. Maybe she assumed he knew.

She was allowing him to hold her; she'd allowed a lot of men to hold her. Maybe it didn't mean the same thing to her that it meant to him.

"Why weren't you talking to me?"

He took the time to take a breath, blowing it out in an almost sigh. "Part of the reason that I became what I did was because I had such a hard time talking, to girls especially."

"You were shy. Santa said you were shy...*you* said you were shy." There was a smile in her voice as she reconciled the two of them together.

"Yeah. I was. I am. But I realized, after you and I talked, that my shyness was really about me. Me thinking about me and what other people thought of me, being afraid of that. It's not something that I've been able to get over overnight. Maybe you haven't noticed, but I've been trying."

"You're doing a pretty good job tonight."

"For some reason, the Santa suit gave me the shield I needed in order to open up and be me. I never really had a problem talking to men. It was always women. And you've been the easiest person to talk to once I get started. The Santa suit helps, makes it feel natural to start."

"Is that why you're wearing it now?"

"That, and I wanted you to know that it was me."

"So, every time you want to talk to me, you have to put the suit on?"

He thought her words were kind of flippant, with a touch of humor. He loved her humor. It said so much.

"Is that going to be a problem?" He truly didn't think it would be.

"I think you look dashing in it."

"That's good to know." His hand smoothed over her back, and he grew serious. "But I don't think I'll need to. The darkness helps too. But I don't think I'll need that either. I think, you knowing what I was, and you seem to be okay with it, although you haven't said...."

"How can I not be okay with it? You seem to be okay with what I've done. And that's much worse."

"I think we had this argument before. And I won. It's not much worse. If it weren't for me—men like me—you wouldn't have a job. So let's just say that's settled."

"I don't think I can agree with that, but I can agree with the fact that what you were is not going to be a problem for me. However, if you don't or can't talk to me...that will be."

She said that last sentence with a bit of insecurity, and he got the feeling that maybe she had had relationships where there wasn't much talking. Which made sense.

"I think there needs to be a balance. I definitely think in order for us to know each other, we need to talk. But I'm not going to say that's all I want. Is that going to be a problem?"

"Not tonight?"

He huffed out a breath. He supposed it was a natural question for her when he was thinking anything but.

Maybe he was putting the buggy ahead of the horse, but he was going to be honest. "I was talking about far down the road, when you're wearing my ring."

She stiffened under his hands, and he figured he didn't just have the buggy ahead of the horse, but he pretty much had the barn and the pasture and the fence and anything that could get in front of the horse ahead of the horse.

"Forget I said that. Just remember, talking is good, but kissing is better."

"I don't know if I agree with that. I don't believe you."

That struck fear into his heart. What she had done had obviously scarred her. Maybe, it had never meant anything to her at any time.

He didn't know if he could change that.

Chapter Fourteen

urgundy got up late deliberately the next morning. Embarrassed.

Ashamed.

Crew had said something about the dark making things easier. She could definitely relate. In the harsh light of morning, it was hard to hide, which is what she had an overpowering urge to do.

She had tossed and turned the night before after she'd walked up the stairs and got into bed.

She'd realized the right feeling, the complete feeling, the warm coming-home feeling that she felt from the very beginning with Crew had gotten deeper and stronger and pulled like a current on her now.

And that feeling? She was falling in love with Crew.

After the embarrassing things she had told him, and admitted to, and knew he'd seen her do, knew anyone could see her do...she had to get away.

The only problem was so far she'd earned less than one thousand dollars from Mrs. Scholz, even though she saved every penny. Since her room and board was included.

She hadn't bought a thing for herself, and she wasn't going to. If she worked another two or three months, she would have enough to go somewhere else, and maybe Race and Penny would help her.

The idea of staying with Crew was just unimaginable.

Falling in love...she liked the feeling. It felt good and right and better than she ever imagined it would be. So much more than what she thought. And she didn't even know how it happened. Other than maybe because of the Santa uniform, she'd let her defenses down, which she had never done before. Not with any man.

Crew was special too. The fact that he had a past made it even more so, but just the fact that he wasn't perfect eased her mind.

Maybe physical perfection was something that most women looked for. It was something she had looked for back when she was young and dumb, but not anymore.

The fact that he wasn't perfect was far more appealing. A major reason he could relate to her.

There were lots of other men who weren't perfect. Men who didn't look perfect, men who didn't act perfect, men who had physical imperfections. Surely, if she could fall in love with Crew, she could get over it and fall in love with someone else.

Her heart rebelled over that thought, but she clung to it stubbornly.

She couldn't stay. She wouldn't stay. She wasn't going to try to figure out how to make it work. She was going to find a man who didn't know about her past, and then she would make sure he didn't find out.

The thought didn't sit well, but she couldn't think of anything else to address the fear that rose up in her every time she thought about how right it felt to be with him, how good it felt to be held while she cried, and how amazing it was that he didn't expect anything more.

Nothing more than to have her head on his chest and his arms around her.

He didn't expect the payment that she'd been conditioned to give.

But he hadn't been shy about saying what he wanted either.

His attraction was just as strong as hers.

As she descended the stairs, Mrs. Scholz was already in the living room. They had all but one section of the shelves cleaned off and taken down, and they were ready to start painting, once they filled in the holes.

Mrs. Scholz was working on the last section. "Somebody slept in this morning. Hope you're in a better mood than that man was."

Mrs. Scholz was back to calling Crew "that man." It must have been a sour morning.

Which made Burgundy smile, glad she wasn't the only one that either hadn't been able to sleep or had woken up with a headache and a rotten attitude.

"He's back to what he'd been before he started talking." Mrs. Scholz picked up a plastic flowerpot, turning it over in her hand before putting it in the pile of donations. "From the way you look, if I weren't mistaken, I'd say you two met somewhere and spent some time together last night. You both woke up with the same rotten look on your faces."

"Good morning to you too. It's a beautiful morning, isn't it?"

If one liked dreary, overcast, cold, brown days. Which Burgundy didn't happen to, but maybe there was someone who did.

"You know where liars go," Mrs. Scholz said with a censoring tone in her voice.

Burgundy almost said she was headed there anyway, but she knew it wasn't true. Through Jesus, God would forgive anything, even what she'd done, even though she felt it was impossible.

"A good attitude makes for a good day, doesn't it?" she said, realizing that she needed to apply that to herself, because she'd woken up with one of the worst attitudes ever.

With that in mind, maybe she needed to think that things could somehow work out.

"That man wanted to talk to you when you got up."

"I'm here now. He can come talk to me anytime."

"I'm pretty sure when he said that he meant for you to go out and talk to him in the barn."

"We've got a lot of work to do in here today, and I'm late. I'll grab a piece of toast and a cup of coffee, and then I'll jump in and start helping you."

"There's coffee in the pot. It should still be warm."

Burgundy went to the kitchen and didn't take long, as promised. She did bring her coffee back out with her, but she'd eaten her toast in about four bites.

She hadn't been fast enough though, because Crew opened the door as she stepped into the living room.

Their eyes met across the room.

She was aware of Mrs. Scholz standing against the wall and almost halfway between the two of them. But she didn't pay any attention to her.

Just the look on his face: concern, hesitancy, insecurity, and adoration that she didn't deserve.

Maybe that was what was on her face too.

The adoration might have gotten her; it would have been hard to walk away from. But it was the insecurity that just killed her.

He didn't need to be insecure. Not about her. Not about what she felt for him anyway. He'd taken his accident, made the best of it. He'd overcome his shyness with determination to speak.

Mostly for her.

He'd bought a ranch and was doing his best to make it work. And he'd honored his commitment to Mrs. Scholz by giving her a place to stay and even helping her with the inside of the house instead of insisting on it being what he wanted, which was certainly within his rights.

There was more; he was deeper and broader and better than any one thing. That was enough.

And to think someone like that, someone that amazing, was looking at her the way he was.

It made all of her thoughts of running seem silly.

Maybe they could figure out how to work this out. Maybe if no one else ever found out what she had been, he would be able to live with it.

"Good morning?" Her words didn't come out nearly as confidently as she wanted them to come, and her breath trembled.

He nodded. "Good morning." His words at least were more confident, and some of the insecurity faded from his face. But he shut the door and walked forward slowly, closing the distance between them.

"Are you okay?" he asked low and quiet, not that Mrs. Scholz would say anything. Underneath her crusty exterior, Burgundy would bet she was as loyal as anyone could ever be. Still, it felt like a private conversation.

"I am." She tilted her head and looked up at him. "Are you?"

"I'm as fine as you are. No more than that."

Who would have thought a man like this, so taciturn, with so much roughness around the edges, could be so romantic?

But there was no question he meant it. The caring concern in his eyes was almost too hard for her to meet.

"Then you just got a whole lot better."

His mouth twitched a little, and he put a hand up, smoothing back her hair and running his fingertips down her neck until it stopped on her shoulder. He didn't try to step closer than arm's length though, as though he thought maybe she needed space.

She couldn't tell how much she appreciated that. She was used to her space being crowded, used to the men in her life pushing for more, used to herself pushing for more, but she wanted what she had with Crew to be different.

It had already been different, and she wanted to keep it that way. Not that she didn't eventually want to have everything that a relationship should. She just didn't want to start out with that. For the first time in her life.

"Glad to hear it."

"I'm headed to the Bible study. I'll leave you two here by yourselves, if you can behave yourselves that long. I expect the room to be taped and spackled so that we can get ready to paint tomorrow when I get back."

Mrs. Scholz came over, walking beside them as she spoke, then going into the kitchen and coming back out with her purse.

"I didn't know you had Bible study today?"

"I just decided to go. I'll see you two later."

Burgundy couldn't keep her brows down as Mrs. Scholz adjusted her purse strap on her shoulder and walked out the door. "Do you think I should go with her?"

"I think she intended for you to stay here," Crew said with another, bigger tilt to his lips. "I think the woman had mercy on me." His thumb skimmed softly over her neck. She loved that his touch wasn't intrusive but almost begged for permission. "I'm going to have to thank her for that."

"You be careful, because I'll start thinking you like her."

"Not nearly as much as I like you." His eyes glinted, and then a shadow passed over them. "Is it okay for me to say that?"

She nodded, biting her lip. "I like hearing it. Is that okay?"

"I should go ahead and try to let you know as often as possible."

She chuckled. "I like you."

He tilted his head, as though he were pondering her words. Finally, he said, "I'm not sure I understand. Say it again."

She laughed. "If you want compliments, just say so."

"I want compliments."

She couldn't believe she was laughing. No alcohol, no drugs, everyone still had their clothes on and she was laughing and enjoying herself. "I can't believe how appealing a man that can make me laugh is."

"Does this mean that I have to use a stick to beat away any man that would try to tell you a joke? I guess we'll have to walk into church late so we miss the pre-sermon funny?"

"I guess so," she murmured. "Although I think it's just you."

"Then you can say, 'Crew, I love it when you make me laugh.'"

"Maybe you should practice a couple more times before I say that."

"The pressure. I can't stand it. I have to be funny *and* sexy. It's too much."

"Nobody said anything about having to be sexy. Just funny."

"Now you're insulting my manhood."

"Really?"

"Sure. I don't want you to just look at me and think 'funny guy.' I want you to look at me and see someone you like whom you can be attracted to, too. I think that's probably a male trait." He lifted a brow, but he said the next words gently as though he wasn't sure whether she could joke about it or not. "Surely, you know that."

Could she admit to knowledge she had learned from things she had done that she wished she hadn't?

"If you don't learn from your bad experiences, what's the point?" he said, as though he could read her mind, but it kind of went with what he was saying before.

"That's true. I don't know if I could joke about it though."

"Why not? Why can't we laugh at stuff? It makes it go down easier."

"Laughter is the best medicine?" she said, thinking she'd heard that somewhere before, but not sure where.

He nodded. "That's right. If you've repented, you've already determined you're going to try your hardest to not do it again, you've already gotten forgiveness, and there's nothing more to do other than laugh and learn."

"Maybe it should be learn and laugh?"

"Maybe. I think they're interchangeable."

She thought maybe he had a point. That was definitely

something she was going to have to work on, because it wasn't going to come naturally.

"I think though, if we're going to keep Mrs. Scholz happy, we better get some work done. What do you think?"

"I agree. Although, I've never painted anything before, so she might not be happy with the quality of my work anyway."

"I've painted plenty of things, and this is probably easier than most of them, so I might be able to give you a few tips."

"Easier?"

"I painted the sides of the ship while it was in the water. That wasn't too bad, although you had to be raised and lowered by rope, and it was a little touch and go there because you have to paint from the bottom up. I've also painted ship railings while we were on voyage as well as helped my stepdad paint vehicles, which is what he did for a living."

"Stepdad?"

Crew shook his head, like he was wishing he hadn't said anything. "I lived with them for about four years during my junior high and high school years. He skipped out. I stayed a bunch of different places, in and out of homes."

He walked over to the bucket of spackling and started to pry the lid open.

The careless way he said it told her more than anything how hard it was to not have a solid home. She couldn't even commiserate, because her home had been the best.

She took the rag Mrs. Scholz had for that purpose and began to wipe the walls.

"So you didn't really have a family?" She'd met a lot of people like that, but it tugged at her heart every time.

It made her feel guilty too, because she did have a family. Her family would be totally ashamed of her if they knew what she'd done. No one in her family would have seen any of it. Her family wasn't that way. They probably didn't even know adult movies like she made existed. They certainly would be shocked to even see one, let alone to see *her* in one.

"You do?"

"Yeah. They don't know what I used to do. They know I left for Hollywood, and I certainly didn't think I was going to end up where I did. The idea was to become an actress. But Hollywood's an expensive place to live, and waitressing doesn't usually cut it. Plus, there's some sneaky advertisements that look like legit modeling and acting gigs but aren't."

She'd fallen for those too. At the beginning.

Then she sought them out.

"So necessity?"

"That, and stupidity. A potent combination." She ran the rag over the wall, over and down, focusing on getting it clean like they weren't talking about her deep and painful drop into sin.

"I don't have that excuse. There was no necessity. It was just what everyone else was doing. I suppose I was kinda young when I started with the drugs and alcohol. Although I have to say the training to be an underwater welder is rigorous, and that probably kept me from going further than what I did. Then I fell in with some good friends. I'd say it's lucky, but I think it's God." He dipped the knife in and pulled putty up on it, filling in the holes of the wall she'd wiped.

"Peer pressure is probably just as bad, especially when you have no home life and weren't taught any values." Unlike her. She'd had all. She'd chosen to turn her back on it. "I could have come back at any time. My parents would always have taken me back. Even now, they'd take me back. It's just a matter of being embarrassed."

"They wouldn't hold it against you?"

She shrugged. "I don't think so. Maybe. My parents love me. There's no question."

"You're still in touch with them?"

"Oh yeah. I just couldn't go there after rehab. I don't want them to know what I've done."

The conversation was interrupted by her phone ringing.

She reached for it, saying, "Do you mind if I get this?"

"Go right ahead."

She set her rag down and swiped her phone. "Hello?"

"Burgundy. It's Rochelle."

"Hey, girl." Rochelle had gone into rehab a few months after she had. She'd been doing well when Burgundy had left. "What's up?"

"I'm done with rehab, and I can't go back. I need a place to go. You're the only one that I know of that has gotten out."

Her voice was almost frantic. It brought back memories of her own, when she had been done with rehab. Done, and determined that she was never going to go back to what she had been, but she didn't have anywhere else to go.

Knowing that if she'd gone back to her old apartment—her old life—she'd be back to doing exactly what she'd been doing before she went to rehab.

She'd needed a new start. And by the grace of God, Race and Penny had given her that when they had contacted the rehab center where she was at saying they had a job lined up for someone who was serious about getting right.

"I don't have a job for you. But I have a place, I'm pretty sure." She eyed Crew, who continued to work. Even if she couldn't get Crew to let Rochelle have a bedroom, Race and Penny would take her. She was almost positive.

"I don't have any money."

"Where are you at?" She didn't have much money either. Probably not enough. Maybe.

"I'm still in Carson City. I'm done today."

"I'll buy your ticket. Hold on. I'll do it now, and you can give me your information." She brought the web up after putting Rochelle on speaker.

Crew had stopped what he was doing, given her a curious glance, and started walking over. She hit the mute button.

"This is a friend of mine. She did what I did. She's done with rehab, and she needs a place to go. Just as I did, and I can't tell her no. If she can't stay here, I'll need to go and see if Race and Penny will let her stay."

"She has a place here." Crew didn't hesitate. And if she hadn't already been in love with him, she would have fallen at that moment.

"Thank you."

"Does she need me to pick her up?" Crew asked, a little hesitantly, and she remembered his shyness. It was almost like it was a barrier, and once he'd broken through, he was fine with her. She supposed it would be something he fought with anyone he didn't know.

"I can go. I'm booking her ticket now." Her fingers were moving over the screen, and her head was down as she spoke. She had just enough money in her account to cover the ticket.

"We'll pick her up at the airport."

Her thumbs stopped moving, and she looked up. "Is that okay?"

He nodded. "Anything for you."

She froze for a second, because she believed...he actually meant it.

Chapter Fifteen

The next day, Crew dropped Burgundy and her friend Rochelle off at his house.

Rochelle didn't have many things to carry, thankfully. After they had gotten inside, he'd taken Burgundy aside.

"I'm gonna take Mrs. Scholz out for lunch. That should give you guys a chance to get settled and have some privacy to catch up."

He loved that look in her eyes. The one that came into them now, that said that what he had done was the right thing, and that she appreciated it. It almost felt like...like she loved him. She had no idea the lengths he'd go to get her to look like that at him.

No one had ever looked at him like that before. Certainly not a girl. None he was ever sober enough to notice. He could hardly imagine the girls he'd been with when he'd been drunk and high had ever looked at him like that.

He'd much rather have a sober look.

Funny that he was strong and whole then, but it was now—when his physical strength was so much worse—that Burgundy found him appealing.

"Thank you." He started to move, to turn away, but she put her hand on his arm.

He tried to remember if she'd touched him before. That feeling that everything was exactly the way it should be was strong and sank in with every beat of his heart. It felt right.

He stopped. "Yeah?"

"Could we talk later?"

Immediately, alarm buzzed through him. He'd never been with a woman who wanted to "talk" and ever had it turn out to be anything good.

"Is there a problem?" He wanted a heads-up.

"No." Her head tilted. "I guess if you don't want to, that's fine."

She sounded hurt. What had he said?

He wasn't going to wonder about it.

He put his hand over hers and threaded their fingers together. It was like a puzzle fitting into place. So smooth and right.

He'd planned on leaving, but he didn't want to before and definitely didn't want to now. Didn't want to let go. Ever.

"Am I in trouble? Did I do something wrong? Are you going to tell me you don't want me anymore?" There. He just laid it all out. All the things he was afraid of. It hadn't been easy, but it'd been easier than he thought.

Definitely easier than worrying about them for the next five or six hours.

"No!" Her voice was still soft, but she said it firmly.

"Is it something else?"

"I just... I just like talking to you. I just... I wanted to spend some time with you. But if you don't want to—"

"I do."

"I didn't want to force you. I just thought..."

"You thought?"

"I thought we kind of agreed that...we...like each other?"

He admired the strength it must have taken her to say that. He certainly hadn't had the gumption. He assumed she wanted to talk to him, just because. Nothing else. Because she'd taken the effort to say that, maybe it meant that she liked him. Truly.

Knowing that gave him the courage he needed to step forward and wrap his other arm around her while keeping a hold of the hand that was still on his arm.

He pulled her to him, and she fit perfectly, felt perfect, smelled perfect. He closed his eyes to better appreciate the feeling that was growing and expanding inside of him.

"I like you. I more than like you. And I'm happy for you that your friend is here, but I definitely want to spend time with you, anytime you have time." He hesitated. Maybe she wanted more. "Do you want to go out?" He wasn't sure exactly what she meant by "talk."

"Not really. I just love being with you."

On one job they'd had on the ship, one of the guys had brought along a book his wife had wanted him to read. It had something to do with love languages.

Everyone on board had made fun of the guy. Because he actually read the book. Of course, he wanted to stay married.

But Crew remembered a little bit of what the guy had said, something about a love language being touching. Which is what he decided his was.

But there was another one, he thought, that had to do with time. Was that Burgundy's?

She'd probably think he was an idiot if he asked, but maybe there was something to that. He ought to get that book and check it out. If he wanted to do right by her, and he did, he probably should at least try to speak her language.

"So far, everything that I've done that you've done with me has been more fun because you've been there. I'll take you over anyone any day. And I'll take you over being alone. So any time you want to be with me, know that I want it. How's that?" It was plain talk. As plain as he could be.

His words made her smile, and she had that look in her eye again. Man, he loved that look.

"You might have to remind me. I might wonder if you still mean it."

"I'll say it every day if you need me to. I want you with me. Any time you can be with me, I want you."

Yeah, she was smiling, looking at him with that look of adoration in her eyes. He felt like he was Superman and could do anything just because she was looking at him like that.

He needed to remember that he was gimped up and washed out. Practically an old man.

That's not how she made him feel.

"Thanks for being considerate and giving Rochelle some time to adjust."

"Let me know if I can do anything for you or pick anything up for you while I'm in town."

"I will."

Crew pulled into the church with Mrs. Scholz. She was all set to help Miss Penny and her daughters with the pen pal ministry that they were starting.

West, Pastor Race and Penny's son who had donated the horses for the Santa Claus buggy, was just coming out of the church.

Mrs. Scholz nodded at him and said good day, but kept walking. They were a little late.

West shook his head. "Sometimes I think I need to be saved from all those happy do-gooders," he said, with more than a little frustration in his voice.

"You get roped into writing to someone on a regular basis?" Crew grinned, enjoying West's discomfort.

"No way. They tried. Well, my mom and sisters knew better. But that girl, Poppy, who should have been named more accurately Peppy, because I don't think she goes anywhere without a smile and wearing the rose-tinted glasses outlook on life which is annoying," he rolled his eyes, "thought she was going to get me to write to not just one person but two. I set her straight. I'm donating horses, that's enough."

Crew laughed. "It must reek at times to be a pastor's son."

"Well, I didn't tell Poppy," he said her name with a little bit of a sneer, "but if my dad had asked me to, I would have done it. Not that I wanted to, but just because I know I owe Dad."

"Not your mom?"

"Mom wouldn't ask."

Crew shrugged. He didn't know. Didn't really have parents so he didn't know what the dynamics were. Just had to agree. "Your dad in there?"

"He is. In his office. Make sure you go in the back way and avoid the main Sunday school room because Mom will get you. And if she doesn't, Poppy will. Avoid her at all costs. She's the redhead."

"Got it. Avoid the redhead. I can live my whole life by that advice."

They laughed, and West strode away.

Crew followed his advice and limped around the church, going in the back door and straight to the pastor's office. He rapped on the door, assuming Pastor was looking for him, since he'd sent him a text saying he wanted to meet.

"Come on in," Pastor called.

Crew opened the door and limped in, shutting it carefully behind him, happy that he'd managed to make it to the office without being recruited to be the other part of a pen pal duo.

"Thank you so much for coming. You didn't have to come immediately, I just needed to talk to you at some point." Pastor Race stood up from behind his desk and came around with his hand out.

They shook, and Pastor offered him a chair. When they were settled and had talked about the weather and how the Secret Santa things were going and how Mrs. Foote was doing, Race leaned back in his chair with his hands behind his head. "I have some ideas I wanted to run by you."

"Shoot."

"Denver told me you weren't sure what you were to do with your farm."

"That's true. I knew it would probably be too much work for me to run it myself, and after a month, I'm sure that's true. This isn't even the hard season."

He hadn't wanted to think about it. He didn't know what he was gonna do to support himself, let alone if he ended up with Burgundy. And then when she wanted to bring a friend, he figured go ahead. It wasn't something he could refuse. As long as he had a place, he'd share it.

He had enough savings to pay for necessities and his mortgage for a year. But that wasn't a lifetime. Far from it. He needed to get something figured out.

"Well, I've been talking to some of my friends and some people who are in public ministry. Also some celebrities who are interested in supporting a rehabilitation type facility." Pastor Race leaned forward, like the idea of talking about it excited him. "Not the first line of defense, but somewhere people can go after they get out of rehab, if they can't go back to where they came from, to learn life skills and to be reacclimated into society. Mistletoe is growing as a tourist town, and there are jobs. This is a good place to be."

Sometimes it just amazed Crew how the Lord worked things out.

"You wouldn't believe what happened today, now that you're mentioning that. Burgundy brought a friend home, who has just gotten out of rehab. She's at my farm right now."

Race's eyes narrowed, like he was wondering how Burgundy knew someone in rehab, but then Crew remembered that Race was the reason that Burgundy was there.

Did Race know what Burgundy had done before rehab?

Crew figured it didn't matter. He didn't think it would make any difference to Race.

But it was something that would make a difference to some people. A lot of people would care if they knew.

"You know what, that doesn't surprise me at all. God often works like that. That's just one more sign that I think we're on the right track. I've got some sponsors lined up. They're coming in two weeks.

I haven't spoken with Burgundy yet, but I have a favor to ask of her." Pastor Race picked up a pen from his desk and clicked the end. "Don't say anything to her. I don't want her to worry."

Crew nodded.

Pastor Race straightened, carefully putting the pen down and setting his hands on the desk, tapping his fingers on it, and pressing his lips together. "Don't tell Burgundy about the celebrities, either, please. I don't want her to be nervous. And I don't want that knowledge to influence her answer of the favor I'm going to ask."

"I understand."

They talked a little more about the logistics of setting a rehabilitation facility up on the farm, and getting donations, and how it could be run. How Crew might be paid and his potential part in it along with Burgundy.

To Crew, it felt like an answer that he'd been waiting for. Certainly not what he'd had planned but definitely something he could do.

Crew did not mention that Burgundy and he were getting close, because there was nothing to say. He certainly wasn't going to go around telling other people when he wasn't even sure that Burgundy and he had anything figured out other than they might like each other.

Two hours later, he managed to escape the church with Mrs. Scholz and without being recruited to be a pen pal to anyone.

It was worth celebrating, so he took Mrs. Scholz to the coffee shop for lunch.

Chapter Sixteen

_S_upper was a little bit awkward.

Rochelle, having been told by Burgundy that Crew knew what they had done for a living, was a little self-conscious and maybe a little louder and more boisterous than she might have been otherwise.

Crew, on the other hand, who had been talking to her just fine without any trouble, had clammed up with another woman in the picture, and it was all she could do to get him to say "pass the salt."

Burgundy laughed to herself more than once over the awkwardness of someone speaking too much and someone not speaking at all. Mrs. Scholz, for once, seemed like she was trying to help, in her crusty old way, which wasn't much help.

As they finally finished, and Burgundy got up to help clear the dishes, Mrs. Scholz said, "Why don't you let me do this tonight."

"I'll help," Rochelle said eagerly.

Burgundy opened her mouth to argue. This was her job after all, but Crew had stood, and his hand was poised above his plate like he was getting ready to pick it up.

"Would you like to take a walk?" she asked over the table and in front of Mrs. Scholz's and Rochelle's opened mouths. It had taken a lot of nerve. Both Mrs. Scholz and Rochelle stared at her.

She stared at Crew.

He looked back at her, his eyes dark and deep. It was hard for her to tell what in the world he was thinking.

"I'd like that. I have something I want to show you anyway."

She couldn't keep her face from twitching with his declaration, and she stepped away from her chair, pushing it in.

"Okay. You guys talked me into it. Thank you so much."

She was used to being forward and had tried hard in the year or so since she'd been out of her old life to curb that impulse, but she didn't try to curb the impulse to take his arm, which she did as she walked by.

It startled him, and he looked down at her fingers on his arm. Touching him felt natural, more natural than anything she'd ever done.

It was a little scary, because she thought she could get addicted to it. And she'd fought so long and hard to kick the other addictions she had. It felt a little bit like standing at the abyss and willingly taking a step.

She was counting on the fact that Crew wouldn't let her down.

She hoped she was counting on truth.

They grabbed jackets and walked to the door.

He opened it for her, and she stepped out into the cool night air.

"It's the first day in February, and that's about the time spring starts around here, or so I've been told," Crew said, like he hadn't just spent the entire meal using monosyllables.

"It's pretty amazing to me that you get away from everyone and it's just us, and you can say anything."

His laugh was self-conscious. "It's pretty amazing to me, too. You're the only woman that's ever happened to me with. I'm working on it, though. I'm sorry I didn't do better tonight."

"There's no such thing as you doing better. You are who you are, and that's good enough for me."

"I want to be more than good enough."

"Really? What exactly do you want to be?"

"Amazing. Awesome. The best." He grinned, and she supposed that was a man. There were a lot of men in her life who had been pretty insecure about a lot of things and had wanted her to assure them, usually about more specific things.

She got used to lying.

She didn't want to lie to Crew.

She didn't want to be a liar at all in her life.

She'd vowed to tell the truth. She wasn't going to go back to lying to make people feel good.

"I think you're well on your way." And that was the honest truth.

She wasn't sure if it was her words or just coincidence, but his hand brushed her hand and his fingers slid in between hers and clasped around them.

"Is this okay?"

That was so new. She wasn't used to men being considerate. Asking.

She was used to the assumption that because she was what she was, anything went.

"I can't imagine that you would do anything that wasn't okay."

He heaved out a breath. "Maybe you don't have a very good imagination."

"Maybe you're not giving yourself enough credit."

"When you talk like that, you make me want to be better. Better than what I know I am."

"Maybe that's what Pastor Race was talking about in church on Sunday. As iron sharpeneth iron?"

"Maybe," he murmured around lips that curved up. "Maybe it has to do more with the things a man will do for a woman that he's falling in love with."

She couldn't stop her gasp.

"I didn't mean to scare you."

"You didn't. You made me happy."

He opened the barn door, and she looked at him. "We're going into the barn?"

"If that's okay. The lights aren't very good, but there are some. What I want to show you is in here."

"That's fine." She stepped in, and he closed the door, the darkness settling around them. She didn't like the dark, and she immediately wanted Rosemary, longed to have her to squeeze against her chest.

She took a deep breath, blew it out slowly.

"Watch your step while we walk over here. I'll get the lights."

He did something, something that wasn't just flipping on a switch but more like putting one piece into another piece, and the lights came on.

She wasn't sure exactly what he'd done, but she didn't think she needed to figure it out, since she wasn't planning on being in the barn without him.

Her eyes swept around the barn floor. What did he want to show her?

It wasn't hard to spot. Two long ropes hung down in the middle of the wide-open floor, from rafters far above, and a board—it looked like a regular board—was hooked to the end of them.

"A swing?" Her heart looped, making her smile.

"Yeah. I thought you'd like to swing with me."

"Like, us together?"

"I guess. I thought I could push you, but I think we could both sit on it. I know it's sturdy. We'll be fine."

There was a little bit of hope in his voice, and she thought maybe that he hadn't thought of them sitting on the swing together, but when she suggested it, that's what he wanted.

She wasn't sure she was ready for that.

That was a lot of weight, and she thought maybe she'd rather do it by herself first.

"Do you think maybe just me to begin with?"

"The lady doesn't trust my workmanship?"

"I do. I just...don't trust me."

"You'll have to explain that one to me, because I don't get it." They'd reached the swing, and he put a hand on the rope.

She looked up at him and grinned. "Okay. I don't trust the workmanship."

"Do you want me to swing first?"

"No. I can do it."

She sat on the swing but then jumped right back up. "Never mind." The thought had just occurred to her that, with her background, he was putting a lot of trust in the fact that she said she'd changed. What if she hadn't? What if she went back to what she was?

He was counting on the fact that she wasn't going to do that.

That was a lot of trust.

Would it take any more trust for her to sit on the swing with him?

No. Definitely not. Less for sure.

"What? You don't want to swing after all?"

Maybe he was trying to keep the disappointment out of his voice, but he wasn't entirely successful.

"No. I want to swing. With you." She turned, looking up into his eyes, sincere.

Maybe she was playing with fire. But she didn't think so. Crew was most definitely not like the other men that she'd been with. Even if he'd done a few things that he was ashamed of, he had a solid core about him that said she could do whatever. That he wouldn't let her down. That he wouldn't push her further than she wanted to go. Which, of course, made her willing to be more free with him. Funny how that worked.

"Will you sit down?" she asked with a little smile.

Not the kind of smile that she might normally have used on a man before, but the kind of smile she used on a man she might be falling in love with.

He hesitated, and that made her wonder if she was pushing too much. "I don't want you to do anything you don't want to. I don't want you to feel pressured."

"Oh, I want to. That's not the problem."

"Then what's the problem?"

"Maybe I want too much." He shook his head, not taking his eyes from her, as he walked around and sat down on the swing. "I want more than I deserve. I feel like everything I have to give in return is not enough."

Her breath caught. No one had ever treated her like she was valuable before. She'd always been a commodity. When Crew said that, it made her feel like he really did feel like she was worth more than anything he had.

Maybe it wasn't true, but she felt like it was.

She held his eyes and moved closer. Then she settled on his lap, her arm going around his neck and shoulders and another arm holding onto the rope.

They hadn't been this close, hadn't touched like this, and it made everything inside of her jump and sway. Her voice most definitely held a husky note when she said, "Is this okay?"

"Exactly what I want," Crew murmured.

She smiled.

"Are you holding on?" he asked.

She nodded. Her throat felt tight. He smelled like chocolate and coffee and fresh air which all combined to form a scent that was all his, one she couldn't get enough of, along with his heat and that powerful feeling of everything being just right.

He started pushing, and her arm squeezed tighter. He smiled in response and pushed more. The rope was long, and one advantage of that was they could swing high.

She'd never swung like that before. She worried a bit that they'd lose control, but Crew seemed to know exactly what he was doing.

Whether it was because of any special skill, or whether it was just the nature of the swing, she wasn't sure. She didn't analyze it. She just enjoyed the feeling of flying through the air.

It wasn't unlike the feeling she had when she was with him anyway. Like she was falling, but a controlled fall, sheltered in his arms, and held steady by his presence.

"It's been years since I've swung. I don't even remember the last time." Her eyes closed, enjoying the wind in her face as they went forward.

"Me either."

"Something made you think of it."

"I just wanted to do something fun with you. And this was just the thing I thought of. Nothing special triggered it."

She turned to look at him, and he had that look on his face, the one he had before, where she felt like he'd do anything for her.

Maybe she had that same look on or something even more deep and real.

It felt like she could tell him anything, and her mouth opened without her thinking. "This is how it feels when I'm with you. That sweeping sensation in my stomach. It feels so good, because I know you're beside me and around me and holding onto me and everything feels right, and all I have to do is just enjoy it."

"You just explained exactly how I feel, only on top of that, I have this driving need to make you smile. To see you happy. And to know that it's because you're with me."

Their faces were close, and his breath whispered across her skin as he spoke.

Maybe it was the feeling of being free, or maybe it was the feeling of the solid man holding her, but everything in her head snapped into place and felt as right as the puzzle pieces that seemed to fit together earlier when he had taken her fingers and held her hand.

She lowered her head. "I want to kiss you."

She could honestly say she'd never kissed a man on a swing.

"I guess we want the same thing then," he said, his voice rough.

She was sure he wanted it; that wasn't a question. She also was sure that the idea that he just wanted to make her happy, make her smile, see her have the very best, made everything different. Different than any other kiss she'd ever had.

She lowered her head as the swing swooped backward and the air pushed her hair away from her face.

He tilted his head, and their eyes met before her lips touched his, and the swing started sweeping back the other way, taking her stomach with it, and making her clutch his neck, her mouth opening and pressing into his, her hair blowing back and shielding both of their faces.

Maybe it was the swing, maybe it was the man. Probably a combination of both.

She'd never had a kiss make her feel like she was flying, hot and wild even though there was no grasping or clasping or fake moaning and groaning that had marked so many of the kisses that she'd shared with so many of the people that she kissed. But it was his soft, gentle kiss that didn't take but gave and made pastel colors float across her brain. Despite the longing, there was no fervor but just a sense that it was exactly right. Perfectly beautiful as she fell over the cliff and into his arms.

Chapter Seventeen

On Sunday when Crew took Burgundy and Mrs. Scholz and Rochelle to church, he was still smiling over that kiss.

He hadn't really intended the swing to be a kissing swing.

He'd thought Burgundy would sit in it and he'd push her. That seemed kind of romantic, something that would be fun. He wasn't really a romance guy, but he was used to improvising to have fun. He did that on the ship all the time, in his old job.

A lot of times, it was competitions—climbing and racing and running and things like that. Whatever could be done on board a ship.

So the swing probably was born out of that.

Still, when she'd suggested they sit on it together, he couldn't believe he hadn't thought of that. A brilliant idea.

And one he'd savored. He hadn't expected the swing to result in a kiss.

He certainly wasn't turning it down. He'd take more. A lot more where that came from.

But he didn't want to push Burgundy. She had a lot of painful issues in her past to get over, and he didn't want her to move quicker than she was comfortable with. As hard as it was for him to wait.

He most definitely didn't want to wait. He was sure she was exactly what he wanted, and he was ready to move on, which meant...

It was too soon to think about marriage. Way too soon.

But he didn't see any other point in hanging out together, if that wasn't the end goal.

Was there another point?

He'd never been one to beat around the bush or to fiddle around. He wasn't interested in a relationship for the sake of a relationship. He was interested in finding a wife.

He had a feeling that Burgundy might feel a little different.

She'd never been courted before, from what he could gather, and maybe the swing was a little bit of that too.

Courting.

Just letting her know that she was worth the chase. Worth him doing something hard for.

Worth his time and effort.

Worth the wait.

She was worth it all.

So maybe he was thinking about all those things and hadn't really been paying attention until he realized that Burgundy, her hand in his and walking by his side, had stiffened to the point where she stopped.

He took another step before he stopped too and looked over.

One look at her face made him think that she was seeing a rotted corpse walking out of church. It made him look.

All he saw on the stoop was just a man he didn't recognize, wearing a suit that didn't fit very well and looking uncomfortable in it anyway.

Until his eyes landed on Burgundy. They shifted to Rochelle, then back to Burgundy.

Those dead-looking eyes narrowed, and he looked at Burgundy again.

He could have described it as a corpse coming out of the church, but more likely, she was looking at someone from her past.

Someone who knew about her past.

Maybe someone who was involved in her past.

Crew hadn't realized he could feel this sick, sharp, curdled-vinegar feeling in his stomach that pinched his throat and shriveled it up like it was pulling away from the back of his mouth.

Maybe it was jealousy. He hadn't even thought about how he'd feel if he was confronted with someone from her past.

It wasn't a good feeling.

But he also felt protective, like he wanted to step in front of her and defend her from everything. Especially from the slimy-looking man with the dead eyes.

He tried to calm himself. She needed to be able to face this on her own.

The man smiled, like he'd found what he'd come for, and walked to the edge of the platform.

Later, Crew wondered if the man had gone into the church, looked around and not seen her, and come back out, because the service hadn't started, and everyone else was headed inside.

They were right at the last-minute rush, and there must have been twenty people milling about outside, greeting each other and moseying in.

Burgundy's hand tugged in his. "I've gotta go. I can't do this."

There was panic in her voice and in the jerky way she yanked her hand, trying to get away from his.

He let go. He wasn't going to make her face anything she didn't want to. She had every right to run until she was ready.

But then, as though her more rational self had taken over, she stopped jerking her hand and straightened.

"Never mind. I guess this is something I need to face, isn't it?" Her head turned slowly to his, and there was so much pain in her eyes he wanted to pull her close and kiss her again, shutting out the worst of the world and cocooning them in their own private place that he'd only just discovered on the swing.

He hadn't shaken his head or nodded, but she jerked her chin up. And then gently pulled her fingers from his.

The pain was still in her eyes, and he didn't want to let her go. Wanted her to know that he was here beside her, behind her, and supporting her in whatever she needed.

The man stood on the stoop, right in front of the door. A crowd gathered in front of him, unable to push through.

Maybe a couple people had greeted him and asked if he needed anything, but his eyes were on Burgundy, and they didn't move.

"Who is that?" Crew asked, thinking that maybe he'd be better able to help her if he knew what was going on.

Her breath heaved in a painful-sounding way, almost wheezing before she blew it out. "I made a lot of movies with him. And his friends. He was usually the director, and the one who bankrolled everything, as well as a participant in most films."

There was that sharp yank on his throat again, and the vinegar felt even worse in his stomach.

Definitely jealousy. But he wasn't going to leave her. He'd promised he wouldn't.

How could she trust him if he did?

He couldn't think about the pain and tried to ignore the ache that used to be his heart as he put a hand on her shoulder.

"What do you want me to do?"

Her head turned, and her eyes landed on the hand on her shoulder. Almost like she couldn't believe that it was there. Maybe she knew how badly he was torn up inside, but he doubted it.

Her eyes lifted to his, humble and grateful. "That's enough."

"Bunny Flame, that's who that is. Look at you in your little modest churchgoing dress, with your old man gimping along beside you. Is that all you can get now? He's as washed up as you are," the man sneered from the top of the church steps.

Crew figured it was a good thing he wasn't inside the church, since there would be that danger of the ceiling falling down on him.

"Did you want something?" Burgundy's voice was soft. It didn't hold nearly the confidence he was sure she wanted it to. His hand squeezed her shoulder. Her backbone straightened.

"I sure do. I heard you got out of rehab and got straight. I didn't believe it. I came to see for myself. I figured if it was true, I could offer you a few greenbacks to lure you back. That would make a good story, wouldn't it? Bunny Flame returns. I'll be the first." The man had rubbed his fingers together when he said "greenbacks," showing the universal sign for money, and he sneered at Burgundy.

"You're wasting your time. I'm out, and I'm done."

There had been some gasps in the crowd as a few started to figure out what the man was saying.

He spoke for a few more seconds, lewdly describing what he expected Burgundy to do with him, and the gasp of the Sunday churchgoers were not as subdued that time. There were several that sounded outraged and outspoken.

Crew stepped forward, not letting him finish. "We don't need to talk like that here. The lady said she wasn't interested. You can leave."

"Lady? That's rich." The man rolled his eyes. "Is the cripple going to do something about it?" The derisive tone left no room as to what he thought of Crew and his inability to walk.

Crew felt a presence beside him, and he did not need to turn his head to know that Denver had stepped up. They'd worked together enough that Crew knew exactly who it was.

Denver would back him no matter what.

But he didn't want to step on Burgundy's toes, if she were going to handle this. So he stood loose and waited for a signal from her.

※

BURGUNDY COULDN'T BELIEVE she was facing this man at church.

Clyde Fisher.

She'd done a lot of work with him. What she said to Crew was exactly accurate. In front of the camera and behind it. He'd played both parts.

And that meant exactly what Crew thought it did.

She couldn't believe he was still standing beside her.

But there was no doubt she could never face the people at church again. Not after what he'd just said. Everyone knew exactly what she'd been.

She hadn't missed the angry gasps, nor had she missed the mothers who tried to shove their children behind them. She also hadn't missed several teenage boys who stepped closer, with interest, she was sure. Wanting to peer at a person who would actually do the things that Clyde had said.

They certainly weren't words fit for Sunday morning in front of the church house. Pastor Race would probably be extremely upset if he knew she had brought all this on his parishioners.

"There doesn't have to be an accommodation. I'm not interested. And that ends it. Now, move so these good people can go in and worship the Lord." Her voice wasn't timid any longer, and she put all of her anger and frustration into it. It came out confident and clear as a bell, ringing across the churchyard on the bright Sunday morning.

Clyde sneered and gave her a derisive snort. "That's all it looks like to me. Looks to me like you brought some of your friends along, and you're starting in the business for yourself. You know I can make you money. We've made plenty of it together before." His look turned sly as he eyed Crew. "That's not all we've done together."

Pastor Race appeared behind Clyde. One hand with long, agile fingers landed on the man's shoulder. "This is a place for sinners. I'm glad you found us. If you want, you can come inside and sit down and listen, or you can go. But you're not to be harassing anyone else in the churchyard."

Burgundy wasn't even sure where they came from, but West and Ethan had casually walked to the bottom of the steps and stood just feet away from Clyde.

Clyde hadn't missed their slow approach, and his eyes went to her, then to the man beside her.

"I guess I know why you're with her. But she's not that good." He said a couple of other things designed to insult Crew and embarrass him in front of everyone. As well as her. To put her down and make her feel like dirt. Like she didn't already feel that way.

Still, he knew he was outnumbered, and words were all he had.

After the first sentence, the men took a step forward, and Clyde walked down the stairs, giving her a couple more crude insults before he walked off, getting in his car and driving away.

People began murmuring and moving. Pastor Race walked down the stairs, saying a few words to his boys.

Burgundy took the opportunity to whisper in Crew's ear, "I can't stay. I have to go. You don't have to take me home. I'll walk."

"You could stay, honey. Everyone here is on your side."

The way he said "honey" made her insides flip in a slow circle. How could they after all that? How could he put such tenderness in an endearment after that as well?

She shook it off. It was probably her imagination. "Everyone?" she asked, knowing without a shadow of doubt not everyone was on her side. There were many people, maybe even half, who would happily tar and feather her because of what she'd done in her past and what she'd brought on them this morning. They didn't want to be faced with that kind of evil as they went to worship the Lord.

They wanted to see little white lies, maybe the occasional swear word, and perhaps a bit of unrighteous anger.

Certainly not the kind of sin she brought to them.

Crew couldn't argue with her, and he must have been able to tell that she was dead serious, because he leaned down and said something in Mrs. Scholz's ear.

Mrs. Scholz argued as well, but Crew just shook his head.

Rochelle turned with her, and they walked together back toward Crew's pickup. She didn't want him to be guilty by association, so she didn't wait for him. She didn't try to touch him or hold his hand, either, when he did finally get alongside her.

She crossed her arms over her chest and looked at the ground, walking as quickly as she could without running. She didn't want to look like she was running away. Even if she were. Because she was.

Chapter Eighteen

Crew supposed it didn't shock anyone when Race showed up at the ranch later that afternoon.

He certainly wasn't surprised. But after he had gotten Race a cup of coffee, and settled him on the living room chair, and Burgundy still wasn't down, he thought maybe she really hadn't been expecting him.

Or maybe she was hiding.

He hadn't seen her since they'd gotten home. She hadn't said anything to him in the pickup. He hadn't pushed, and she and Rochelle had disappeared upstairs as soon as they got home.

Rochelle had seemed sympathetic and maybe even a little angry, but Crew hadn't thought that Rochelle would be trying to talk Burgundy into anything crazy.

Rochelle had seemed happy for Burgundy that she might have found something...he hated to call it love, maybe he was afraid to call it love...with him.

Regardless, when she hadn't come down, he excused himself from Race and walked up the stairs.

He'd wanted to do it in the hours that they'd been home, but he had figured that he needed to respect her privacy and her right to be alone if she wanted.

She knew by now, surely, that if she wanted him, he was there.

It'd been hard to wait and give her space, but he still felt it was the right thing.

He didn't know what he was expecting when he knocked on her door, but he supposed it wasn't to have it opened by a dry-eyed, stone-faced woman, already packed with her suitcases sitting on her bed.

It was Burgundy with all her shields back up.

He hated it.

He searched her face, looking for a crack in the armor, knowing that there was a sensitive and caring woman under that façade, and wishing with all his heart that Clyde's egregious breach of anything resembling sane human interaction hadn't caused her to hole up again, hiding behind her shell and her walls.

The suitcases on her bed pulled his eyes, and he studied them for a bit before he looked back at her.

Rochelle wasn't in the room.

"You're leaving?"

It seemed obvious, but he didn't know what else to say. How did he break into that conversation? Could he just say, "I don't want you to go?" Did he have that right?

She nodded decisively. "Everybody knows what I am now. I won't do that to you."

"Do what to me?" He wasn't playing dumb. He really didn't know.

"You being an outcast in the church. Did they kick you out? Did the posse come yet to tell you that I had to go or you wouldn't be allowed to stay?"

"You've met Race and Penny. They're the ones who invited you here. They love you."

"They knew I was in rehab, but I'm sure they didn't know why.

They had no idea what I was. There are privacy laws, and they couldn't have known. I certainly didn't tell."

"It won't matter. I promise. Plus, even if it does matter to them, it doesn't matter to me."

Crew wasn't entirely sure she was correct. Race had talked about a rehab center, and he talked about having it for people like Burgundy. Had he not realized that he was offering it for former adult movie stars?

Crew could hardly believe that could be true. But she was right; there were privacy laws. And really the only way Race should have been able to find out what she had been was through Burgundy. If she didn't tell him, he must not know.

"It will matter to you eventually. When you're embarrassed and shunned because of me. I mean, this is the modern age and everything, and maybe in a big city, we could get away with this, but you can't live in small-town America with a past like mine."

"Maybe you haven't been in small-town America long enough to know what you can and can't get away with here. I'm telling you it won't matter."

"You're not the one that has to live with that every day. I'm going to have to look in everyone's eyes and know what they know about me."

"You would have to do that wherever you go."

Her face fell, and he felt bad for saying it. Even if it was true. She couldn't run from her past. She had to face it.

His shoulders slumped, and he looked away. It wasn't his job to tell her that.

Not to mention, she already knew it.

If possible, she looked even more dejected now than she had when he walked in. He figured he might as well tell her why he'd come.

"Pastor Race is downstairs. He'd like to talk to you."

Her head snapped around, and her eyes shot to his, betrayal on her face. "You let him in?"

"I'm telling you. He loves you as a sister in Christ. He wants the best for you. I promise."

"Easy for you to say. He doesn't know what you've done."

Crew nodded. She was right. Race didn't know.

He didn't ask but just grabbed her hand. "We'll rectify that right now." He tugged and started walking down the hall.

"No! That's not what I want."

"It's what I want. We'll start on equal footing. If he's gonna condemn you, he can condemn me too."

She didn't exactly fight him, but she didn't exactly come eagerly either as he walked down the stairs.

They'd barely made it to the bottom of the stairs. As soon as Race's head turned to look at them, Crew started talking.

"Before I got saved, I drank all the time, I was definitely an alcoholic. I couldn't function without alcohol or drugs in any kind of social situation. I grew sober long enough to work, long enough to study to learn to do the job that I was doing, but as soon as it was five o'clock, I was drinking. I didn't go anywhere without it. That led to drugs, which gave me a better high. I slept around. I couldn't tell you how many girls. Anyone who was willing. I wasn't picky. I was always drunk or high, because I couldn't talk to girls otherwise, and it wasn't just one girl at a time. And of course, right along with that, I was a regular at the adult bookstore. I had the discount card. I was there at least once a week, sometimes more. I rented every movie they had and bought most of them. I had magazines, and I subscribed to a bunch of different websites. You name it, I was in it. It was like that for years. Until I met Denver at a job, and we became buddies, and I went to church with him, and I took Jesus. After that, I left it all behind."

He dragged Burgundy over with him until they stood in front of Race, who looked a little shell-shocked at being bombarded with all that at one time.

"Burgundy seems to think it would make a difference, but even though I lived about as raunchy in life as a person can live, I never got paid for sex, but I did just about everything else. I haven't done anything since I walked the aisle. And if God will forgive me, I know he expects you to too. Whether you can or not, I don't know. But I'm not afraid to admit any of that, because I know it's under the blood."

He stood in front of Race, one knee slightly bent because his hip was killing him, but he wasn't going to sit down, and he wasn't going to give up. If this was what Burgundy needed for him to do, it's what he would do.

"Burgundy seems to think that what she's done has made a difference. To you. And whether or not you will accept her. I say what she's done isn't any worse than what I've done. She might have made the movies, but I bought them. I watched them. I gave them an audience." He almost added that that was how he was able to recognize her, because he'd seen her in a movie. But maybe there were just some things that were even more personal, too personal, to share.

He didn't want to make this any harder on Burgundy than it had to be. It was about him. His sin. His grace, and his forgiveness.

Not hers.

She had to come to grips with her own.

At this point, Race was nodding.

"I see. I wondered why you were throwing all that on me." The man lifted his eyebrows and blew out a breath. "It's been a day. Almost enough to make me want to pick my scalpel back up and step back into the old operating room. High-stakes life-or-death operations are a little less stressful than what I've dealt with today."

Crew grinned, despite the seriousness still in his chest.

Beside him, he thought maybe Burgundy relaxed just a little.

"I guess that really wasn't what I had come to talk to you about, Burgundy. I guess I was going to touch on it, because you left without saying anything, and I just want to make sure that you know you are not the one in the wrong this morning. It was the man who was standing on the step being so vulgar and disgusting." Pastor

Race grimaced as though he hated even the memory of what Clyde had said.

He shook his head. "I like to think of our church as a hospital for sinners. It's where we go to get better. It's not where we go when we're perfect. That's heaven. I gave up my scalpel and working on physical hearts to stand behind a pulpit and work on spiritual ones. Period. Again, no one is perfect, including me and you and you." He looked them each in the eye.

"You didn't come to kick me out of the church and tell me I couldn't go back?" Burgundy asked, not contritely, but almost with a defiance in her posture.

"No. Never. There is no sin too great that God won't forgive it. How could I judge you more harshly than He does? I have no right. I didn't speak anything into existence. Holy smokes, I can't even speak my sermon notes into existence whenever I've lost them. I have no right to refuse to forgive something that God's already forgiven. And neither does anyone else. And as far as I'm concerned, that's the way our church operates. If people don't like it, they can go somewhere where they have perfect people to be around." He snorted. "Good luck for them finding that."

"Oh." Burgundy seemed to kind of wilt, and Crew stepped closer to her, touching her side with his and putting his arm around her shoulder. She leaned into him, and all the tension that seemed to be keeping her upright drained out.

She melted against him.

"Maybe this isn't the time to talk?" Race asked.

"No. Please. You made the trip out here, go ahead."

Race twisted his coffee cup. "The first thing I wanted to say is that Crew and I had been talking about turning this farm into a type of rehab center. Where people can go when they've been released from rehab, but they don't have a place to go home to or they're afraid to go home for fear that they'll fall back into whatever it was that they were trying to get out of."

His eyes glowed with excitement. "I have a whole bunch of ideas, and Crew and I have already talked about it. But I wanted to run it by you, because I was hoping that you would help. You've been there, and you've done that." He didn't flinch away from the hard words but said them matter-of-factly. "My wife and my daughters and other ladies in the church will give you a hand. But they haven't been there like you have. And you can reach people that we can't." His eyes dimmed a little. "I can't guarantee a salary. Not right now. Which leads me to the other thing I wanted to talk about."

Burgundy had straightened a little, and it wasn't hard to see that she was shocked at what Pastor Race had just suggested.

It also wasn't hard to see that she was seriously considering it.

"Go ahead, I'm listening."

"I was hoping next Sunday in church, you could tell your story." Pastor Race put his hand up as Burgundy straightened and drew a breath in to speak. "Only as much or as little as you want. Whatever you think will help people. I just think, first of all, that whatever you've been through, other people need to hear it. Sometimes, I think we're insulated from the outside world. We don't realize the evil and the wickedness that's going on there, because we're in our nice little church bubble. I also think sometimes you don't realize how big God is, that he's bigger than the evil that's out there. If we don't know how big the evil is, we can't really know how big God is, now can we?"

The question Race asked was perfectly logical, but it wasn't something that Crew had ever really thought about before.

He thought maybe Burgundy was considering the same thing, because it didn't seem to be something that she considered either.

"You don't have to. No one is going to kick you out of the church if you don't. Since that seems to be a worry of yours."

Crew snorted. Normally Pastor Race was very serious, but he definitely was joking there. Even Burgundy smiled.

"In fact, let me ease your mind. I've never, in my entire life, seen anyone kicked out of a church. I have seen pastors ask people to leave, but normally those are people that the pastor can't get along with, and instead of the pastor growing himself and trusting the Lord to lead him, he takes the easy way out and gets rid of what he thinks the problem is. Unfortunately, usually the problem is in his own heart, and no problems have been solved by what he did."

Nobody said anything to that. There didn't seem to be anything to say. Other than that was logical too.

"Do you need some time to think about it? I can come back, or you can let me know." Race stood up and set his empty coffee mug on the end table.

He took one step before Burgundy said, "No. You don't have to come back. I can tell you now. I'll do it." She paused. Then she looked over at Crew. "Would you stand with me?"

"I'd be honored to."

Chapter Nineteen

Burgundy went to her room while Crew walked Pastor Race out.

She'd agreed to talk next Sunday, but that didn't mean she wasn't still leaving. She'd known when she and Crew had been talking before and he kissed her that she brought a lot of baggage with her. Baggage that would hurt him, in a lot of different ways.

Today was just an example of that. It was going to happen over and over and over again. For the rest of her life.

She didn't want to subject Crew to that. Leaving was her way of defending against that. A soft rap at her door had her jumping off her bed, grabbing Rosemary, and clutching her to her chest.

She had to face him sooner or later. She might as well face him now.

She straightened on her bed, swallowed, and tossed her hair. She could do this.

"Come in."

Rochelle opened the door and stuck her head in. "You want to talk?"

Disappointment cut through her chest.

Funny, she was leaving him, but she couldn't wait to see him—longed to see him more than anything. Even if it was to break up with him. Just to see his face.

"Sure. Come on in."

Rochelle walked in and closed the door carefully behind her.

"It's been a day," she said by way of greeting.

Burgundy stroked Rosemary. "It sure has. But I guess I deserved it, and I kinda asked for it, and I kinda thumbed my nose at this kind of thing for years. It catches up to you."

"I want to be sober, and I want to quit porn, but I'm not a hundred percent sure that I actually want to do the whole God thing."

"It's hard at times. Sometimes, I want to quit. I'm not going to lie."

"Why are you still doing it then?"

Burgundy's fingers stroked over her elephant. Rosemary wasn't soft anymore. She wasn't new. She wasn't anything that would be valuable to anyone else. But Burgundy loved her with a fierceness that she couldn't even explain. Maybe with the fierceness that she would have loved her daughter had she not killed her instead.

"God is the only explanation I have for what he brought me out of. And how I came out. If that's true, and God really is as great as what everyone says, that he made the world, and you and me...I can't do that. Can you?"

It was a rhetorical question but not one that anyone ever actually asked themselves.

Rochelle's forehead wrinkled. "You're asking if I can make a person? Sure, I can get pregnant. My body will grow a person."

"Do you know the chemical reactions that takes? Do you know the biology behind it? Could you do it in a lab? Could you form a person yourself and have them have a baby?"

"Of course not. Don't be ridiculous."

"Well, God's got one up on you," Burgundy said, with a little bit of sarcasm in her voice.

"Okay. Fine. But what if we evolved?"

"Prove it. You prove that we evolved, and I'll prove there's a God."

"But I can't. And neither can you."

"Exactly. Either one takes faith. And if you believe in evolution, if you put your faith in that, then me coming out of porn was just a coincidence. And I'm sorry, too many things had to happen for that to have happened just so. And yet here I am, and it feels like there's a higher power guiding me. I can choose to ignore that, and I can choose to believe something else, but it still takes belief."

"I guess you have a point, but it's not enough of a point for me to want to give up everything and do the Christian thing. You have to, like, love your enemies, which I'm not doing, and you have to, like, be nice to people all the time, and that's not me either. And then there's the whole you can't swear and you can't drink and you can't do anything fun anymore."

"Where did all that fun stuff get you up to now?"

"But I'm out of that."

"You think you can do a little bit and get away with it?"

"Probably not. But I don't have to become a Christian."

"You're right, you don't. God gives you free choice. I certainly can't force you into anything."

Rochelle lifted a shoulder. "I don't know how I started arguing religion. That's not what I came in here to talk about."

"Probably my fault. I'm sorry. I guess God's love is so amazing to me, I want everyone to feel it. I'll shut up about it now. You can talk."

Rochelle looked like she was gonna say something more, but she closed her mouth over whatever it was and shook her head. "I just want to say, in the short time that I've been here, I've never seen a man look at a woman the way that man looks at you. I thought I heard you with your suitcases, doing what you said you were going to do when we walked in the house. I just want to tell you how stupid you are. As a friend." She grinned a little to ease the sting of that. But she was dead serious, Burgundy had no doubt.

"A life together takes more than looks."

"That man would do anything for you. He'd give up anything, he'd sacrifice anything, whatever it took, I'm telling you right now, that's not something to take lightly. I mean, lots of people have said 'I love you' to me. And you know exactly what they meant. They loved me as long as I was doing what they wanted.

"But even when that man thought that you were going to be leaving him, he stood by you. He still loved you. And he'd give you anything right now. I bet, if you said you were leaving, but he could go with you, he'd walk away from this right now. Follow you. Bet you anything."

"Why would I want to do that? I would hate that."

"I'm just saying." She lifted a shoulder and held out a hand. "In our business, you know what we usually get. A few words, maybe some promises, but nothing means anything. Nobody keeps them. Nobody means them. Yet you've got yourself a man that means what he says and will prove it by his actions. You can test him, or you can trust him. I suggest you trust him."

Rochelle had sat down on the bed, but she stood now. "Miss Penny talked to me on the phone a little bit earlier. She wants me to come live with them for a while, although she said that there might be a rehab facility opening up in the area. She said maybe I could get a job there. If not in town. She'd help me. I thought I'd move out and give you and Crew a little bit of time to spend together without me sitting between you. I think you need to stay."

She walked to the door and put her hand on the knob.

"But I guess God gives you free will, so I have to too." She smirked a little, not unkindly, but just the way someone did when they threw one's words back in one's face.

"I hear you. You better not go anywhere."

"I'm not. I'll be in Mistletoe if you need me."

"Thank you."

Rochelle stopped, halfway out the door, and turned and looked over her shoulder. "No. Thank you. I don't have another friend in the world who would put the money out for my ticket like you did. And who would have gone and gotten me and brought me to their house. Don't you think for one second that I don't know that I owe you."

CREW LAY UNDER THE TRACTOR. The motor was spread out in pieces on the barn floor back in the corner on the opposite side of the swing.

He'd been working on teaching himself the basics of motor repair. He already figured he could open a welding shop without too much trouble. The suffering that he went through because of his accident wouldn't be enough to keep him from being able to make a living there.

But he figured it wouldn't hurt to diversify some. He didn't need practice welding.

He'd done it underwater for almost fifteen years, and he knew it forwards and backwards.

Although, if they turned this into a safe haven for people who'd graduated from rehab, he wasn't sure where that left him.

He wasn't sure he wanted to be doing anything here if Burgundy ended up leaving.

At least it sounded like she was going to be staying until Sunday. But she still hadn't said anything to him. And he didn't know where he stood, other than beside her on Sunday morning.

He'd promised, and he'd be there.

He wasn't the kind of person who said something, and didn't remember it, or didn't hold to it.

The lighting wasn't that great in the barn, and when a shadow fell over the tractor, it was pretty noticeable.

He went from being able to see a little to not being able to see anything.

He moved his head, curious as to what was going on.

"Do you have a minute to talk to me?" Burgundy's voice came from around the seat of the tractor.

"Always." He slid out from underneath, careful not to get any splinters in his back from the wood floor.

If he were going to do this on a regular basis, he'd need a cement floor and a creeper. At least.

He straightened up, brushing off his back as far as he could reach.

His stomach churned. He wasn't sure what she could want. He kinda suspected it wasn't anything good. Maybe she'd changed her mind about what she told Pastor Race she'd do.

He figured when he had gone back in the house, and she wasn't downstairs waiting on him, that she still wasn't wanting to talk to him.

Kinda obvious.

He'd almost started getting used to the disappointment.

Expecting it even.

He came around the back end of the tractor. She met him halfway and didn't stop. She put her hands on his shoulders, and he had to blink a little.

"Don't." He put his hands on top of hers to stop her from coming any closer. "Don't, just because you know what I want."

"Aren't I allowed to want too?" Her hair flowed around her face. She shook her head, and he swallowed hard, meeting her eyes.

"I was really getting the impression today, from the way you were avoiding me, that you didn't."

"I'm sorry. I needed a little bit of space to think. I know that this is going to make up the rest of my life."

She paused. He didn't insert anything into the silence.

"I didn't want to make you deal with the pain."

"I guess that makes you less selfish than me." He was going to let her talk, but he had to point this out. "Because after all, I'm not exactly whole, in case you haven't noticed. This isn't going to get any better. It's going with me wherever I go. The rest of my life. If you're with me, you're going to be stuck with it."

"You think I care about that?"

"I guess I could ask you the same thing."

"True."

"Don't hate me, but I've been thinking you ought to invite your parents for next Sunday."

She flinched, as he'd expected her to.

"I think maybe I can live the rest of my life without them knowing."

"You probably could. It's up to you."

"Can I just say I'll think about it?"

"You can do anything you want."

"Well then, I will." She pressed against his hands, and he let her go. She closed the distance between them and pressed her body to his. "Even this?" she asked with a lifted brow.

"Especially this," he said, sliding his arms around her.

She laid her head on his chest, which wasn't exactly what he wanted, but he pulled her closer and marveled again at how right it felt for her to be there.

"I just wanted to make sure we're okay," she said softly. "I'm sorry that I kinda had a bobble there. I probably will have a few more before we get straightened out. I hope that's okay."

"I can be patient with you, as long as you're patient with me."

"I haven't had anything to be patient about yet."

"It's coming. I'm sure. On rainy days, when I'm really sore, I get pretty short-tempered."

"I haven't noticed."

"I imagine you will."

"Will you help me with what I want to say on Sunday?"

"You know I will."

"I wasn't sure. I wasn't very good to you today." She looked down. "I kinda shut you out, and I'm sorry."

"Thanks for apologizing. It makes it better. Easier. Because, yeah, that did hurt."

He couldn't even believe he was admitting somebody had hurt him. That wasn't exactly manly. Regardless, she seemed okay with it.

Didn't seem to think less of him because he wasn't completely strong.

Maybe that was what love was, recognizing that the person you loved wasn't perfect and not holding that against them.

Speaking of which… He cleared his throat, his hands tightened, and he rested his cheek on her head. "I admire the way you stood up today at the church, and I'm always proud to stand beside you. No matter what you decide, I just want you to know, I love you."

Her breath froze, and she stiffened under his arms.

His heart stopped—had he made a mistake in telling her—but only for a few seconds, then it started again, faster this time.

She lifted her head, looking up at him. "I love you too. That's why I was leaving. I know it doesn't really make sense, but it's true."

Her face was sincere, her eyes wide, and he knew exactly what she was saying.

"I understand. Believe it or not, I understand. Sometimes, love means letting go, especially if you think you're hurting the other person by holding on."

"And sometimes love means standing beside someone, even though it hurts you, and even though it's not easy, and even though the rest of the world thinks you're crazy."

"Is that me or you that the rest of the world thinks is crazy?"

"Both?"

They smiled together. Then she reached up, or he reached down, or maybe they both did each.

Regardless, he kissed her.

Chapter Twenty

"Don't peek." Crew took Burgundy's hand and led her in through the barn door.

She giggled, the sound slipping around his heart, and squeezing.

"What could this be?" she asked with another sweet giggle, sounding for all the world like an innocent little girl.

His heart squeezed at what she'd been through, and what she done, and he wished he could give her experiences like this for the rest of her life. She wanted so badly to put all the junk of her life behind her, and he wanted to be able to help her. Wanted to be able to help her be "normal."

"Just a little bit further, and you'll find out. Watch your step." He led her around the loose board in the barn floor, slipping his arm around her waist.

She leaned into him, trusting.

It was such a difference from what they'd had before, the lack of trust and the outright suspicion and his inability to communicate. They came so far he could hardly believe it.

"This had better be good," she said, but there was no threat in her voice.

He could be showing her an old, broken clothes basket, and she would be still happy and giggling, even if she were a little confused.

He guided her around the corner and into a soft pile of straw that he'd been meaning to sweep up for a while, but just hadn't gotten around to.

Whiskers had found it before him, and she had birthed her six babies there.

That's what he wanted to show Burgundy.

"Are you ready?"

"I've been ready for a long time now," she said, with just a hint of dryness in her tone.

"Oh, did you say you wanted to wait longer?"

"Are you going to let me see today?"

"Are you going to quit being so impatient?"

"This is me being patient, trust me."

"Really? I think I found an area where you can use some work."

"There are a lot of areas where I could use some work." There was a hint of sadness in her tone, and her voice had dropped a little. But then she lifted her head and her mouth turned up, brightening the part of her face below his hand which was holding her eyes closed.

"Now?"

He moved his hand away, and she opened her eyes blinking. Looking around, at the barn, and the empty hayloft, and the old hay bine that sat in the corner half torn apart.

"I don't see anything?" Her brows furrowed as she studied the hay bine. "You're not showing me that old piece of equipment are you?"

Meow.

It is just a whisper of sound, a little squeak, but it was enough to draw her eyes down.

He wished he could freeze the look on her face – the look of wonder and gentleness and caring and absolute adoration, before she dropped to her knees.

"Oh, my goodness! Oh, they are darling!" She shook her head a little and peered up at him. "I cannot believe I just used the word 'darling.' But I meant it."

Her head went back down, and her finger went out to touch between the ears of the mama cat.

"They are the most adorable things I've ever seen." She leaned forward. "And what is your name sweetheart?" she asked, stroking between Whiskers's ears.

"I've been calling her Whiskers. Pretty unoriginal, and if you want to change it, feel free. She came with the house, and I don't know what her name was before. I suppose Mrs. Sholz would know, but I never thought to ask."

"Whiskers. That's perfect. My goodness you're a busy mama." Her finger went to each kitten, and she counted softly. "There's six?"

"That's what I got."

"I think this one is going to be white. And look, this one's white with orange on it. They're all different colors. And none of them look a bit like their mom, who's a tiger striped gray."

"Guess that happens sometimes. She and the father must have been a real hodgepodge of genes."

"That makes things interesting, doesn't it?" She seemed to droop a little, like she was thinking. The thought ran through his mind that maybe someone in her situation...but no. Surely not.

She looked up. "I have two babies waiting on me in heaven. That's where Rosemary came from."

He wasn't exactly sure what she was saying; he wasn't exactly sure he wanted to know. But, he wanted to love her despite the hard stuff, or through the hard stuff, or with the hard stuff.

This was going to be a chance to prove it. He'd probably have a lot of chances to prove it.

"Miscarriage?" he asked, trying to not sound hopeful.

She shook her head, sadly, but watching his eyes. Her expression said she wanted to know if he was going to love her through the hard stuff.

This seemed like a good time to tell her.

He dropped to his knees and took her face in his two hands, running his thumbs under her chin. "I love you. I love you now, I love you yesterday, and I'll love you tomorrow. No matter what."

"Even that?" she whispered, the hurt stripping her tone and making it raw.

"Anything. Anything at all. I'm always going to love you."

"I don't know how much to say tomorrow."

"Just say what you're comfortable with."

"Some of it you might not even know."

"It doesn't matter. I'm telling you, so you know it's not going to change how I feel about you, and what I want for us."

"What's that?" A little tremor crossed her face. Maybe the idea of being tied down scared her. It seemed like it might.

"I want us. Together. For the rest of our lives. That's what I want."

"You don't know what you're saying."

"I know exactly what I'm saying. I want you."

It was easier to say those words than what he had thought. Of course talking to her had just gotten easier and easier. He felt more comfortable with her than he ever had with anyone, even most of his male friends.

"Don't forget, I have a past too."

"There's a difference between watching and participating."

"Not really. Plus, it's all water under the bridge."

She hadn't said anything in return to his declaration of love. It pinched at his chest and squeezed his heart. He couldn't expect reciprocation. He needed to be willing to give without getting anything in return. That was part of loving.

Finally, she stroked a kitten and said, with her head down, "If you say that to me enough, I might start believing it."

"Believe it. Because I mean it."

She looked back down, as her finger gently traced one meowing kitten, the single one that wasn't eating contentedly from its mother.

Her breath huffed out a little, before she looked up at him. "You know, I love you too."

His chest expanded. He hadn't realized he was holding his breath. "I guess I do."

"Sometimes I feel like I'm floundering, and you feel like such a rock."

"I'm not. Although I feel stronger with you beside me. Like, as long as you believe in me, I can do anything. I know that's not true, but that's how I feel. Maybe that doesn't make everything turn out perfectly, and I'm not saying that I don't feel like I couldn't fail, but I feel like it wouldn't be as bad as long as you're still there."

"I'll be here. I've never said that to anyone before, and it scares me just a little, puts a little tightening pull right in my heart, but I want to do that. I want to be with you." She took a breath. "I can't even believe that this opportunity is here, I don't want to let anything happen to it. I don't want to admit the things I've done, afraid that you'll turn away."

"You just admitted something, and I'm not turning away. In fact, I was thinking about that kiss, and thinking that maybe we ought to practice some more."

She laughed. "Thank you. Thank you so much for looking at me and seeing something better than what I am. You make me want to be that person that you see."

"I see the truth. I see what you are. Maybe you just don't see it yet."

"That I guess we're here for each other. I'll stand beside you, make you feel like you can do anything, and you look at me and see what you believe I can be, and I think that's about the best thing we can do for each other."

❄

SUNDAY MORNING BURGUNDY held Crew's hand as they walked into church. He had squeezed it three or four times already just since they had stepped through the doors, knowing she was nervous. Maybe he could feel her trembling. He probably couldn't feel her knees shaking, but they were.

She'd never been this nervous before in her life.

Not with anything.

The beginning of the service went quickly. She couldn't see how crowded it was because they sat in the front – Crew sitting close with his arm around her.

She couldn't believe he'd told her that he loved her. Her parents had told her that when she was growing up, but it wasn't something they said a lot, and she hadn't talked to them much since she'd left.

Ashamed.

Love was a word that got thrown around a lot in the circles she ran in, but didn't mean anything.

She wanted it to mean something. She couldn't believe God had given her this opportunity to build something new, and she wanted to grab it with both hands.

And, if she could help someone else who had done what she did and wanted out and wanted to be able to put the past behind them, then she wanted to be able to do that, too.

That she could be with Crew, they could have it on his farm, and this could be her life...it was almost unbelievable.

"Are you going up?" Crew's voice came in her ear.

She jerked her head. She'd totally missed the introduction. "Is it time?"

"He just introduced you." Crew was grinning, and it made her smile. Oops.

But he didn't seem upset or like he was pushing her to hurry, and she appreciated that.

Her fingers shook around the cards that she held, not that she really needed them, it was her life story after all, she just didn't want to forget anything.

Pastor Race shook her hand as she reached the pulpit, and then he walked away and she stood behind it, turning and facing the congregation.

It was packed. There were a lot of people she didn't recognize, although plenty that she did. Denver and Natalie, Ethan and Ruby. Mrs. Sholtz, who was smiling, and looked as proud as a grandmother.

Her eyes stopped roving as she saw her parents in the audience.

Who had invited them?

Her stomach dropped. And her hand clenched, bending the cards.

She couldn't do this. She couldn't admit what she'd done. Not with them here.

But as she studied her parents' faces, somehow, she realized they knew. This wasn't a shock to them. All this time, she'd thought they had no idea. But gossip travels like wildfire in a small town, and if someone had gotten a hold of it, then yeah. Her parents knew.

Her mom looked sad, but her dad sat straight. Even though he didn't look exactly proud of her, he didn't look like he hated her either.

There were more men in the back, dressed in business suits, that she didn't recognize.

Then, off by himself at the end of the very back pew, sat a man she did: Rafe.

Her director and costar of so many different movies.

What was he doing here? Had someone invited him?

If her stomach dropped when it saw her parents, it tried to run away now. She did not want Rafe here.

Then guilt pinched her. Why not? He already knew all the things she done. Maybe, *maybe* the Lord had him here for a reason. Maybe it was his turn to leave that life behind and get out.

The church had been silent for a while. She cleared her dry throat and started off in a small voice. "I'm Burgundy..."

"And she's a porn star," Rafe yelled from the back.

There was a gasp that went through the congregation, and people's heads swiveled, first to Rafe, then back to her.

Could what he said be true? That was the question on all their faces.

She heard the whispers, saw the shocked expressions, and her feet wanted to follow her heart right out the door.

But this is what she'd come for. This is what she was going to admit. He wasn't screwing anything up. Not like he thought.

She forced her chin up. There was no turning back.

Although this wasn't what she'd been expecting.

She could improvise. She was good at improvising.

So she did.

"Porn star. He's right." Her voice came out clear. She forced herself to speak louder. "Only he forgot one thing – the ex in front of it. I'm an *ex* porn star. Jesus saved me. And I want to tell you how He did it."

That shut people up anyway. The church had become as quiet as it was on a Monday morning.

"I don't think you're going to find anyone as bad as I was in the Bible. People often say Mary Magdalene was a prostitute. Maybe she was. There was Rahab as well. She was in the lineage of Christ, but she was a harlot. The Bible clearly says it. It makes no apology for it. I suppose the woman at the well is another one that possibly might come to mind. She had been married five times. The man that she was living with wasn't her husband. They were all worthy of Jesus's attention. And worthy to be in God's story."

Yeah, people were looking at her now. She didn't hold rapt attention, and she hadn't persuaded anyone, but there were less openly hostile looks. And mothers had loosened their death grips on their children.

"I think sometimes in our society, we think that there's okay sin, and there's not okay sin- the sins that are really bad." She wasn't a preacher, but she knew what she was saying was true.

She met her parents' eyes, so hard. "But in God's eyes, sin is sin. I do think, some sins leave deeper scars than others, and I would never suggest anyone do what I've done, but I used to think that I was too bad for God to want to have anything to do with me." Her mom's face crumpled and her father pulled her close. Burgundy bit her lip and, needing his strength, found Crew. His heart shone on his face and in his eyes.

She smiled, wanting to thank him for giving her what she needed, but pushing forward. Later.

"After all, even though God mentioned those ladies and through them God showed us how our lives could be used for good and God had a plan for them, they weren't as bad as what I was. I guarantee you none of them had done the things I've done. But, sin is sin. And God doesn't quantify."

She was as sure of this as she was of anything. It's what had helped her.

"If a blue-blooded heiress in a department store steals a purse just for fun, just for the thrill, that's as much of a sin as the housewife who buys herself that same purse off the internet and lies to her husband about it, which is just as much of a sin as the husband who gets angry and yells at his wife because she spent money they didn't have. And I get it, it's not 'dirty' sin," she said, putting air quotes around "dirty," "Like porn."

There she said it, and she managed to keep from looking up to see if the ceiling was going to fall down around her. She couldn't keep from pausing though. She wanted to brace herself if that was going to happen.

It didn't.

She continued. "And yeah, he's right. I was porn star. For years. On a weekly basis I made movies. I'm ashamed of it. And I wish I could change it. But I have repented, which means I've turned away from that, and I'm *not* going back. God's forgiven me. Jesus took my sin, he carried it to the cross with him, and God doesn't see that sin when he looks me. He sees me just as white as snow, because I've been washed in the blood of the Lamb."

She stopped there, because she kind of got choked up. It was inconceivable to her that her sin – as big and ugly as it seemed in her mind and memory – was gone.

"I can't fathom a love where someone would sacrifice so much for someone as filthy as I was." She had to put that in past tense. Had to. Because it was gone.

"I think that's what makes our God different from any other god. He loves us. And He shows it. Even when we don't deserve it. But the really compelling thing about that is, God loves us that much, and then He wants us to go and try to love people the same. With that same deep unrelenting love that doesn't care how badly you've been wronged, or how badly someone is screwed up, He wants us to love them anyway."

Her eyes swept over the crowd, but she couldn't linger on her mother, who was crying. Her dad's hand rubbed her upper arm as her head leaned against his shoulder.

That sight tore at her heart.

She never meant to make her mother cry.

Just that alone would make her go back and make completely different decisions if she could.

Impossible.

So, she was going to use it for good. Was going to do everything she could with the experiences she'd had to help others – people who couldn't be helped by men like Pastor Race, who needed her, in her brokenness, to meet them in theirs.

God could use her life for good; she could see it clearly now. And she was going to let Him.

Her eyes rested on the front row, where Crew stared at her, looking at her like she was so much more than what she knew she was. The admiration in his eyes, and the feeling that he found her worth loving, spurred her on.

"It's been my dream, to somehow help others who are like me. To somehow do for them, what was done for me. There were people who looked at me, and didn't see what I was, but saw what I could be. I want to look at other people like that. I want to see the best in people. I want to see better than their best, I want to see their potential. I want to love them with a love that doesn't quit, until they believe they're worthy of that love, and they reach for that potential that I can see."

She turned and looked at Pastor Race. He stood, smiling at her.

No, not smiling. *Beaming* at her as he walked over.

He took the microphone and explained a little bit about what the church was interested in doing, and about how she and Crew were going to help, and provide the facilities for a place for people to stay after rehab, eventually getting work and becoming valuable members of the community.

The men in the back who Pastor Race said were business people he'd invited, were smiling. If she were any reader of people, she would say they were impressed.

Her mother blew her nose, but the look on her face was relief and love. Her dad sat straight, and while she knew that there would always be hurt in his heart for what she had been, she thought there was pride in his eyes for what she could become.

But the most important man was sitting in the front row, and he had never quit looking at her like she was so much more than what she was, and she couldn't stand beside Pastor Race for another second.

She walked away from the pulpit and down the stairs, but she didn't have to walk over to him, because Crew met her there at the bottom, picking her up and twirling her around, while the congregation clapped.

Epilogue

West Barklay watched the congregation rally around Burgundy and Crew.

Two more unlikely people, he couldn't imagine. But it was pretty obvious they loved each other.

It was also pretty obvious that Burgundy was shocked speechless, when Crew got down on one knee. A circle of people formed around them.

Thankfully West was tall, so even though he was in the back he could clearly see as Crew spoke sweet words to Burgundy, and she started to cry before she held her hand out for the ring, and he slipped it over her finger. Her "yes" rang out in the sanctuary. Crew stood and hugged her again.

West didn't allow his lips to turn up in a sneer. He was truly happy for them, but he did find it a little hard to believe in love.

He'd never seen anyone love each other like his parents, except for maybe Race and Penny.

Maybe his brothers had found love.

Okay maybe there was such a thing as love, but not for him.

People converged on the couple, and Poppy led the way.

He watched the bounce in her step and the bright smile on her face that seemed to just light up the entire room, and shine from within her.

She had that glow that people who were perpetually happy had.

It matched the darkness in him. Maybe that's why he didn't like to be around her, because there were things that liked to hide in the darkness and didn't want the light to shine on them.

Not that he was extremely wicked. He just had things he'd rather not talk about. Things that had happened when he'd been in foster care before Race and Penny had adopted him, that had marked him.

Poppy had never had anything like that happen to her. She'd lead a charmed life, with no little bumps or bruises, and definitely no deep darkness.

She was the kind of person that fascinated him and repelled him at the same time.

He took one last look at the happy couple, thinking as he watched them that they'd be married by Easter. They looked like they couldn't wait.

He slipped out the door, through the vestibule and walked outside into the February night. Valentine's Day wasn't that far away. It was a depressing day.

Everybody was so happy with their lifetime loves, and he didn't have anyone.

Not that he wanted anyone, not that he was looking.

Except he did.

He was so deep in thought he almost ran into a woman who was standing on the stoop.

She looked vaguely familiar, although painfully thin, with a head that seemed too big for her frail body and her hair looked odd, like maybe she was wearing a wig.

Three small children clutched at her legs, and she held a tiny baby in her arms.

She was so skeletal, he could hardly tell what exactly looked familiar. Maybe her eyes?

"West?" the woman whispered, her voice hoarse and weak.

"Yeah?"

She knew him. He should know her. But he didn't. Did he?

"It's Minnie. Remember me?"

It took him another three seconds before he remembered. She'd been in that same foster care home that had given him all the bad memories.

"Minnie?" He looked around at all the children and then back at her. Maybe the answer was obvious, but he asked anyway. "These are your children?"

She nodded. "You were so kind to me. I was hoping you'd help me now."

Somehow, he wasn't sure how, maybe he hadn't shut the door tight, but laughter rang out just then. Laughter he would always recognize, and that would always wrap through his heart and chest like warm chocolate on a cold winter day.

Poppy's laughter.

"You want me to help you?" What in the world could she want help with?

Minnie nodded. "I want you to take my children."

Join Jessie's list and be the first to know about new releases and sales on her books!

Read Dreaming of Her Snowed In Kiss, the next book in the Cowboy Mountain Christmas series where Poppy and West are enemies and opposites, but they see a side of each other they didn't realize was there as they work to help a mother dying of cancer. Keep reading for a sneak peek now.

Sneak Peek of Dreaming of His Snowed In Kiss

Poppy Kyle slowed her car to a crawl and gave the old rickety bridge a second look.

She wasn't a naturally positive person, but she'd worked hard the last few years to train herself to always see the good.

Most of the time, it worked.

She bit her lip as her finger tapped on the steering wheel. Positive thinking wasn't helping her to see this bridge in any light other than rotted and old and about to fall into the admittedly placid-looking river below.

The river wasn't exceptionally wide or deep, and the bridge wasn't terribly high; still, maybe it was conditioning since childhood, or maybe it was just a natural inclination, but the idea of falling into it as the bridge collapsed made her keep her foot on the brake and her finger tapping on the wheel.

She lifted her eyes. West Barclay's house and barn were two hundred yards on the other side of the river.

She could smell the steaming meatloaf and almost taste the mashed potatoes that were packed in newspaper and sitting in a box in the back of her car along with three other casseroles that could be frozen or cooked later this week.

She supposed Pastor Race and Miss Penny would be extremely disappointed in her if someone were to find her parked alongside the road, halfway back to town, with the meatloaf and mashed potatoes half gone and crumbs in her lap.

Her stomach rumbled, almost as though putting up an argument in favor of losing her position at the church.

Even if it was volunteer, the idea of not being dependable didn't sit right.

She shoved the idea out of her head, less appealing for the food aspect, maybe, than for the idea of not having to drive over that bridge.

Her finger hadn't stopped tapping. She leaned forward, looking up at the sky, like that would help anything.

She kept hearing about a "storm of the century" coming. Next week. But in her experience, the weather station liked to exaggerate things. They went wild and crazy with their green crayon any time it rained and even wilder and crazier with the white one when it was time to snow.

Not that Arkansas saw that much snow.

But she hadn't always lived in Arkansas.

She sighed. The sky hadn't given her any answers, not that she expected them. Looking out through the windshield, she scanned the picturesque Ozark Mountains that created the backdrop behind West's house.

Pretty.

Beautiful, actually.

Although she hated to give West Barclay any more credit than he deserved. Or his house.

He treated her like an annoying insect—a gnat flying around his head. One he put up with but would prefer to swat away.

Her brain wanted to get stuck on that track, but she pulled it back.

Positive thinking.

Anyway, regardless of how West treated her, he was in over his head with his new houseguest and her four children. Which was why Poppy had a car full of food for them.

Unfortunately, her car was on this side of the creek. In order to get on the side of the creek where West, his guest, her children, and his house was, she had to cross that rickety old bridge.

Tempted to get out and visually inspect the bridge, she stopped with her hand on the latch.

What would a visual inspection help? She wasn't an engineer.

Even an engineer couldn't predict with infallibility whether or not the bridge was going to collapse.

Maybe she'd be better off to say a prayer and have faith.

Lord? Am I supposed to die today? Maybe You could let me deliver the food first?

Holy smokes. She hadn't even thought of that. She'd have to cross the bridge twice. Once on the way over, and once on the way back.

Consider West's pickup.

Maybe it wasn't the Lord speaking to her—He should be talking about lilies of the field rather than pickups—but it was definitely a voice of reason.

His pickup was much bigger, and she assumed much heavier, than her little compact car. Probably it would be an accurate assumption that if the bridge could hold his pickup, it could hold her car too.

Maybe it was the prayer, maybe it was the voice of reason— although she truly believed that God was reasonable and she did not find reason and prayer mutually exclusive—she felt her foot lifting off the brake pedal and sliding slowly to the gas.

She wasn't exactly an expert on driving, and she was kind of torn. Should she go slow and stay on the bridge longer, causing less trauma with the slower speed? Or should she go as fast as she could, taking the chance that she might hit a bump and come down hard with the bouncing, giving undue pressure on what looked like old, rotted timbers?

Deciding moderation was always a good choice, she closed her eyes and pressed on the pedal.

Wait a second. Old rickety bridge or no, she was almost begging for trouble to drive with her eyes closed. They snapped back open.

She laughed at herself.

She trained herself to be happy, yes, but she hadn't completely conquered the common sense she'd been born without.

What seemed reasonable and obvious to everyone else seemed like a brilliant discovery to her, years after other people had figured things out.

Like driving with their eyes open.

She knew it; she just forgot sometimes.

Her front tires hit the old timbers of the bridge and began to rumble across.

The thought that she could point the steering wheel straight and still close her eyes tugged hard at the back of her mind, but she kept her lids up. She would be brave.

She could be both happy and brave.

Maybe having problems to work out was good for her. Always in the back of her mind was the knowledge that she could end up like her mother. After all, she'd gone through the same horrifying experience.

Just because she hadn't fallen into a deep depression right away didn't mean it couldn't happen.

She wouldn't let it.

It felt like years before her front tires hit solid ground on the other side, and she let out the breath she was holding. The food had made it safely across, and so had she.

Now all she had to do was go back over the bridge on her way home.

It didn't take any time at all to pull up to the house and grab the hot food. She'd come back for the casseroles in a bit. It was February, just a few days before Valentine's Day, and even though it was Arkansas, it wasn't hot.

As she climbed the porch to the small house, she realized with the pan of food in each hand, she wasn't going to be able to knock on the door.

What sounded like a muffled thump and a scream on the other side of the door made her wonder about the wisdom of whether this was a good time.

If they wanted their food hot, it had to be a good time. Also, she really didn't want to have to drive over the bridge three more times instead of one, so she was going to deliver it right now despite any inconvenience.

Another three thumps in quick succession had her pulling her lip in and biting down on it. It sounded like maybe the kids had taken over in there.

Maybe she could help.

For the woman and her kids who were staying here and not necessarily for West.

Using her elbow, she rang the doorbell, hoping it worked.

She couldn't hear whether it rang or not.

It felt like forever that she stood waiting before using her elbow to ring again.

She'd given up and was looking for a place to put the pans in her hands down so she could knock when the door jerked open.

West, with a screaming baby in one arm and a crying child holding onto his left leg, stood facing her.

Poppy had been a Christian all her life. She'd been taught not to laugh at another's calamity. That seeing someone else suffering shouldn't make her smile. That she should love everyone and not wish ill on anyone.

Maybe she was arrogant, but she thought, usually, she did a pretty good job on those.

Still, seeing West so overwhelmed with the crying baby and the clinging toddler and the yelling that was going on behind him, she couldn't help it.

She smirked.

"I'd really like to send you away, because I don't want to see happy people right now, but if you're holding food, you can come in." West's eyes had narrowed, and while his words, spoken above the crying child, were not terribly kind, they did represent the type of relationship that she seemed to have with him.

Not hateful; they didn't hate each other. But not friendly either. Kind of a jabbing, poking relationship.

Her smirk fell right in line with that, and his annoyance at her happiness was typical as well.

Apparently, West preferred to be around sour, grumpy people all the time.

She wasn't going to go back and undo all the work she'd done just to keep West happy.

Plus, she highly suspected that he wouldn't be happy anyway, no matter what she did.

He said he picked on her because she was like Pollyanna, but she thought it was her in particular, and not happiness in general, that he didn't like.

"It's hot. You can eat it right now."

He stood back, allowing her plenty of space to pass and saying without words that she was welcome to come in as long as she stayed away from him.

Not a problem.

She walked past and stood in the living room, looking around and trying to figure out which direction to go to get to the kitchen, as the door clicked closed behind her.

She looked over her shoulder as West scooped the child that was clinging to his leg up in his other arm while trying to bounce the baby in his right.

"Follow me," he said, not unkindly but not necessarily friendly either.

There were a couple of trucks and some kitchen utensils scattered through the living room as he walked past, taking a right and walking into the kitchen. No sign of the woman whose children they were, but the two small children that he wasn't holding stood back against the wall, wide-eyed and staring at her, a stranger, walking in.

Her heart tore at their forlorn expressions.

"How's their mother doing?" she asked, raising her voice to be heard above the crying baby.

"Not good," West said matter-of-factly, turning and looking around at her as he said it, his face not giving away anything.

He had to be sad. She was sure he was, but he was definitely the kind of person that was not comfortable sharing his feelings. Happy or sad.

"You can set them on the counter."

Poppy did, and then she turned, intending to tell him she had more casseroles in the car that she would carry in.

But her eyes hooked on the child in his arms. Not the baby who was still crying, but the little one who had been clinging to his leg. He had one dirty pudgy fist stuck in his mouth and was chewing on it like a nervous habit, which sent a pang through her chest that a one-year-old would even have a nervous habit. His other pudgy fist rubbed his eye like it was past his nap time.

Poppy didn't have children of her own, but she'd spent plenty of time in church nurseries, among other things, and had a lot of experience with young ones.

She lowered her head a little, so she wasn't looking at the child head-on—that seemed to be less intimidating in her experience. Then she smiled, not a full, big smile showing lots of teeth. That, too, seemed to intimidate small children. Just a little smile, and she ducked her head even more.

"Are you hungry?" she asked in a soft, sweet voice.

The child looked at her suspiciously, and then West's eyes

opened wide as the little boy took his fist out of his mouth and leaned his whole body toward her.

She didn't bother to look at West to ask permission. They'd spent enough time in church and various activities bantering with each other that she felt comfortable with him, even if she didn't think he liked her too much.

He wasn't going to deny her taking a crying, fussing child out of his hand.

"It looks like it's nap time for him?"

"Past," he said shortly.

"Garrett pooped his pants."

Poppy blinked and looked at the doorway where a serious, sober-faced boy with what appeared to be dried egg on his cheek stood staring at her.

She nodded. Okay. He seemed to consider that important information. She would too.

"Was that just now?"

The little boy shook his head at the same time West answered.

"No, I think Warren is saying that's why we don't have Gabriella down for her nap. Or fed. Because there was something more pressing that I needed to take care of than a screaming baby. Not that I would have thought that were possible."

"Of course. Poop. Or fire." She refused to allow the shudder that went through her to pull her thoughts in the direction they wanted to go. "A fire would be the only other thing that would be more pressing than a screaming baby."

Poppy slanted her eyes at West, only half kidding. She'd never been able to exactly joke about what happened to her, but she wasn't going to allow it to cloud her life. It would throw her into such a deep, dark depression she would never emerge.

Like her mother.

West snapped his fingers and pointed. "I hadn't thought of that. But you're right. Fire would be worse." He seemed to think for a second. "*In* the house fire. *Out* of the house fire, not more urgent."

"Yeah. We could let the barn be burned down. As long as there aren't any animals in it."

"There are. But unless I could find someone to watch the children, I wouldn't take that chance."

Okay, she didn't like the idea that someone would have to choose between saving the life of an animal and saving the life of a child, but she did agree that the children were more important.

"You take care of her." She nodded at the baby, who must be a girl, even though she had a blue sleeper on. "And I'll feed these guys. If that will help."

West eyed her. He didn't look relieved exactly, almost skeptical, maybe.

Yeah. Their relationship hadn't exactly been super friendly.

Not her fault, Poppy told herself.

"Appreciate it," West said eventually, holding the baby in the crook of his arm as he rooted through the cupboard, she assumed looking for a container of baby formula since she saw the old one lying at the top of the overflowing trash can.

"All right, boys," she said, drawing out the word "boys." She was pretty sure from what she'd heard at church there were three boys plus the baby. "Let's get our hands washed, and we can sit down and have some lunch." She made a goofy face at the boy in her arms. "You guys hungry? I have mashed potatoes." She said "mashed potatoes" the way she might have said candy bars, because in her experience, kids love mashed potatoes.

The one in her arms stared at her along with the older boy West had called Warren.

This might be harder than she was expecting.

Sign up for Jessie's newsletter! Get a free book, access to exclusive bonus content, get fun and funny updates on her life on the farm and more!

A Gift from Jessie

View this code through your smart phone camera to be taken to a page where you can download a FREE ebook when you sign up to get updates from Jessie Gussman! Find out why people say, "Jessie's is the only newsletter I open and read" and "You make my day brighter. Love, love, love reading your newsletters. I don't know where you find time to write books. You are so busy living life. A true blessing." and "I know from now on that I can't be drinking my morning coffee while reading your newsletter – I laughed so hard I sprayed it out all over the table!"

Claim your free book from Jessie!